RISE OF THE

HUNTERS I

2nd Edition

By Jonathan Solis

With Illustrations By

Aldi Fauzan

Novel Horizons 2021

Rise of the Hunters Volume 01
2nd Edition

First published by NOVEL HORIZONS in 2020
in the United States of America

ISBN: 978-1-955391-02-3(Paperback)
ISBN: 978-1-7345185-6-6 (Hardcover)

Written by Jonathan Solis

Character Design by Faiz Usman
Illustrations by Aldi Fauzan

Novel Horizons
www.NovelHorizons.com

TABLE OF CONTENTS

PROLOGUE

The year 2035 marked the unofficial end of the world's darkness.

The year when the "good guys" won and the "bad guys" lost. A year of celebration and a year of reflection.

It was time for the sleepless warriors, the hunters of the Darkness, who had pushed back against the darkness in secret since time immemorial, to finally rest.

Their mission completed, their goal met, the ones known as "Hunters" could finally breathe easy, safe in the knowledge that this was the end and that no one would ever need their help again.

A saddening thought, but also one that brought them immeasurable joy.

In the year 2035, the Hunters laid down their spears and never picked them up again. Fading into the shadows without ever coming into the light. Their story complete with no one to tell it.

As it should have been.

"Hm…"

Closing the book and flipping it over, a man in military clothes with multiple medals bouncing on his chest, looked at the cover which read "A History of the Hunters: Dawn Breaks."

There was nothing but a symbol on the cover which, according to the book, was the emblem used by these "Hunters". An emblem comprised of a bronze forward-facing wolf with a golden outline that made it feel simple, yet powerful.

The book was a popular work of fiction and had been ever since its release, despite the fact it toted itself as a "non-fiction" work which was what caused it to be initially condemned by some readers until being reclassified as fiction.

One of the Commanders friends had recommended the book to him and, although he wasn't usually one for fiction, the Commander couldn't help but enjoy the work. Unlike most pointless, unrealistic pieces of fiction, the details within the series were surprisingly detailed, the emotion feeling too raw for a simple piece of literature. Which made it immediately more interesting to him.

The way the text read, it was almost like the author was writing an autobiography, a true history of an organization that had actually existed, which would have given some credence to the work being "non-fiction" except for the fact that the Commander knew that there wasn't nor had there ever existed an organization called "Hunters". A fact he was sure of due to having the clearance to learn about the world's deepest, darkest secrets and mysteries.

In fact, it was that particular authority that had brought him into the middle of nowhere, into one of the few undeveloped lands left in the world.

Following a recent excavation to develop some land in a backwater region, workers had begun going missing under mysterious circumstances with no trace left behind.

Drones were sent to investigate, and while they captured multiple ancient symbols that adorned the walls of a discovered tunnel, eventually they too vanished as their remote-control operators lost contact with them.

"I suppose the locals' warnings had some weight to them…" muttered the commander as he closed the book and recalled the letters sent to the excavation company.

The people who had lived on this land for centuries referred to the cave in question as "Hell's Jail" due to a widespread belief that a great, ancient evil was sealed within its walls.

It was said to be an entity so terrible that its release alone would bring forth great calamity and change in the world, setting humanity back hundreds of years.

Which sounded like most supernatural hogwash many of the remaining "natives" like to tell the Commander, but unlike all the other times, there seemed to be something happening on these grounds that had warranted his personal intervention and inspection.

Upon arriving at the scene, the commander was immediately greeted by the other soldiers who'd been posted on site, just in case things got violent with the locals. Their numbers having increased greatly once the report of missing peoples had been verified.

His superiors were of the mindset that these disappearances were the work of the more extreme protestors of this project, which honestly made more sense to them then the "ancient evil" theory. Making it once of the few moments he agreed with them.

"Any word from the scouting team?" asked the commander as he lit up a cigarette and took a long, pensive draw.

"No, Sir. We lost contact with them."

"Gunfire?"

"Yes, Sir. Although we only heard the echoes from the cave. Their comms died as soon as they entered this area here."

The Lieutenant took out a small round object, which came to life and produced a light blue, semi-transparent map of the cave. It showed all the details, including the destroyed remains of what had once been a door, but the Commander's attention was immediately drawn to a certain symbol... or what was left of it.

"Wait."

Zooming into it, the Commander's eyes went wide, and he immediately took the book he was reading out of his pocket.

"Sir?"

"Lieutenant. Are the markings there not unlike these?"

Flipping to the "codex" page in the back, which was for readers who enjoyed more in-depth details, the Commander pointed to a wolf head symbol that, according to the book, was used to mark areas as "Hunter-Only" zones.

"They are uncannily similar, Sir. But... this is just a book. A popular fiction one and a personal favorite of mine, but fiction nevertheless."

Shaking his head, the Commander marched to the cave entrance with two armed soldiers flanking him on his left and right.

"It should be here."

Running his fingers down the wall, the Commander scoured his memory to recall the "protocol" followed by Hunters when marking areas and, sure enough, eventually, he found an unnatural series of groves Which upon cleaning the wall, revealed another mark.

But this one wasn't the one he was expecting. No, the etching he found there was one that made his blood run cold. A blood that had flowed unwaveringly hot through countless wars and missions, blood that burned passionately in the face of innumerable atrocities and horrors.

The mark was the one found in the last few pages of the last book in the "Hunter" series. A special mark that signified the most glorious victory of the Hunters and the completion of their quest.

The mark of the howling wolf.

But, before he could do much more then process the information, a dark, echoing laughter erupted from the cave. Which was followed by a darkness that began oozing out of the cave, like a viscous liquid, generating multiple yells from everyone who saw it.

The Commander, taking out the book again, stared at the shadows as they crept toward him and stood silent. He knew that if this was what he thought it was then no amount of running would save him.

Instead, he took out his knife and, in a rapid series of swipes, marked the wall over the howling wolf.

As he did so, the now desecrated symbol began glowing a golden yellow before a loud howl exploded outwards from an unknown source.

The howl caused the shadows to pause and the Commander could have sworn he heard a growl emanate from them, but no sooner had the howling stopped did the shadows spring back into action. Although instead of proceeding slowly and methodically like before, now they whipped outwards like violent tentacles, snatching and flinging whatever they could ensnare, consuming all in darkness.

"Hunters, huh?"

Removing the safety from his gun, the Commander pointed the gun at the shadows and spit out his cigarette.

"Open fire!!!"

Hundreds of laser rounds struck the shadows but seemingly did nothing. The rounds phasing through their target as if it wasn't there, but the flying bodies of his soldiers affirmed to the Commander that it indeed wasn't just a hallucination.

His eyes narrowing, the Commander stared Darkness in the face as it continued closing in on him and despite the fact he accepted his fate, he continued his assault as the numbers around him quickly dwindled.

Without relenting or even taking a single step back as the shadows grew closer, The Commander let out an explosive battle cry as the tendrils started latching onto him and in an instant, he was engulfed by the blackness as one of the arms slammed into him.

Leaving nothing behind except for the last book he'd read.

1

PARANORMAL HUNTER: AIDEN

"Everyone! Stay clear! Stay away! This is a potentially paranormal area!!"

Waving his arms wildly, garnering strange looks from all passersby, a young man wearing a bandanna, with semi-reflective glasses, a padded plaid shirt and cargo shorts tried desperately to "protect" everyone from what he had decided was a dangerous "paranormal" tree.

At La Vida high school there were a few supernatural mysteries that made their rounds across the school which included a certain "love" tree and as a member, or rather the only member, of the paranormal research club, Aiden Elrod made it his business to unveil the hidden secrets of these oddities.

Which included, if deemed necessary, eliminating them using his vast "knowledge" of the paranormal.

"Alright, Spirit tree. I've heard stories about how you eternally bind people together under this idea of 'love'." Yelled Aiden as he took out his "paranormal sensor". "But you can't pull the wool over my eyes! I know what you are doing is nothing more than emotional manipulation. Now, admit to your crimes and go peacefully!"

Whipping out a poorly made, poorly drawn badge which had a cute dog on it and the word "Hunter" written underneath with sharpie, Aiden continued staring at the tree in order to intimidate it to reveal itself.

"What's he doing?"

"Don't mind him. Just keep walking."

"Ah, the weirdo is at it again."

Ignoring the words of the people passing him, Aiden got to work to quickly tape off the area which, according to his tireless research, was the tree's "effective range".

While many would consider the act of "making people fall in love if they confess under the leaves" a fairly harmless or even helpful thing, Aiden saw it as an unnatural manipulation of human emotions.

And while he had never witnessed the tree's "powers" first hand, he had heard enough to come to the conclusion that it needed to be purified.

"Your days are numbered." Muttered Aiden, as he took out a glass bottle that had a small cross on it. "No more unnatural relationships, no more of your sadistic emotional manipulation!"

Emptying the bottle on the roots of the tree, Aiden expected there to be some sort of steam or smoke rise up as the water purified the foul entity, but when it uneventfully soaked into the ground, Aiden realized he was fighting an enemy much stronger than he originally anticipated. Meaning he would need to resort to more powerful methods and quickly, too, in case the tree decided to retaliate.

"If holy water won't work... how's this!?"

Thrusting his hand into his pocket, Aiden threw out a handful of salt and expertly formed a salt circle around the tree. His hours of practice doing the act paying off as he created a near perfect circle.

"The Ancient method of hindering the supernatural! The all-encasing salt barrier!"

Nothing.

Clenching his teeth, Aiden was shocked to see such resilience, but also began doubting himself, questioning whether or not he had the right culprit. It could be that the real tree was using a dummy or scapegoat, which in Aiden's mind, sounded like something such an agent of darkness would do.

"Excuse me, young man. What do you think you're doing?"

A teacher walked up behind Aiden and he tensed up as he slowly turned around with a fistful of salt still in his hands.

"N-nothing." Said Aiden weakly, as he pocketed the salt.

There was no point in explaining what he was doing, no one understood the paranormal like him. Very few people even knew or bothered to know about it nowadays anyways.

"I noticed you watering the tree. While I admire your desire to properly care for our school's foliage, especially one that is so famous, I can't say I approve of you blocking it off like this."

"Sorry, I just wanted to make sure I was doing everything right."

"Hmmm. I also want to point out that while plants do need vitamins and minerals, I wouldn't recommend salt. Although, if you are taking this much interest in the tree, are you perhaps hoping to make it look exceptionally beautiful because you plan on making use of its legend?" asked the teacher with a sly smile. "It's an interesting approach, the tree may help you out if you help it. I do like it."

The teacher laughed to himself and Aiden chuckled with him but suddenly stopped as he thought about something.

What if the trees effective range was wider then he thought?

What if his attempts to purify the tree were working and, in a last-ditch effort, it had used all its power to attract a teacher to him, just to stop him in his tracks?

Shocked by this revelation, Aiden looked back at the tree that simply waved gently in the wind, its leaves rustling and narrowed his eyes.

"Next time…" he threatened, as he began packing up his stuff, knowing that he couldn't continue with school staff nearby.

"Try mulch... and more water next time!" added the teacher with a wave as he smiled brightly, before looking around, suddenly confused, and continuing down the sidewalk.

Walking away after packing up, Aiden headed back to the "club room" which was really only a small, old supply closet with a singular window that he was given simply because of his persistence. The space serving as his headquarters, lab and place of peace.

* * *

"History of the Hunters: Moonlight Howl, a History and Codex to the Hunters Method."

Aiden handled the old, hard to find, book gently before placing it softly in his bag.

One of his personal favorites due to being a wealth of knowledge when it came to more advanced paranormal combat techniques and with more detailed, specific supernatural combat methods, he normally would spend hours studying the contents of the text but today, he didn't have time to sit down and read.

So, with a long sigh, Aiden put away all his "Hunter" supplies as soon as he got to the "club room" and got ready to head home.

Locking the door behind him, Aiden pocketed the key before heading down the hallway with a sigh when suddenly, a leg appeared from around a corner and knocked his legs out from under him.

Hitting the ground with a dull thud, his stuff flew out of his backpack, scattering all over the floor.

"Well, well, well. If it isn't our local Exorcist."

A loud, deep voice echoed throughout the empty hallway and Aiden looked up to see a familiar but unwelcome face smirking down at him.

"So, Aiden. A little birdie told me you were talking to Lilian today? Hm?" The newcomer asked as he kicked aside one of Aiden's books before squatting down in front of him.

Sweat dripped down the side of his face as he looked at the man smiling menacingly at him.

Aiden then tried to get off the floor without answering, but a foot from behind slammed him back onto the ground, causing him to let out a sharp cough.

"I-I haven't even seen her today." Struggled Aiden, as the person stepping on him put more weight onto his back. Constricting his breathing.

"Oh, really? Hmmm. Well, I guess he was lying, but just in case you decide not to listen to my warnings, I suppose I should give you some supplementary lessons to show you what happens if you decide to talk to her again!"

Grabbing his hair, the teen pulled Aiden up and slammed his face into the tiled floor, sending a wave of dull pain through it which roared through his spine, all the way down to his toes.

The bully's name was Clark Caloway. He was a popular, well known athlete for the school who was predicted to be one of the best in the academy's history.

Because of that, he had authority, respect and was virtually untouchable because not only did the teachers protect him, so too did the principal who was obsessed with high school sports and would do anything to make her school's team number one.

This included giving top athletes exemptions from classes they were failing, which under normal circumstances meant being suspended from competing.

"She talks to me, I can't do anything about it!" complained Aiden, as Clark jerked his head up.

"Then how about you tell her to get lost? Hmmm? Ever thought about that?" scowled Clark. "You being around her, it keeps making my life harder. She never pays attention to any-one else while you're around and you're ALWAYS around."

Slamming Aiden's face back down to the floor again, Clark told his lackey to get off his back and, within seconds, Aiden was lifted off the ground and held eye to eye with the consid-erably taller Clark.

This routine was fairly normal now and Aiden had gotten used to the abuse, since he was used to facing scrutiny from people due to his particular hobby, but this particular event only started becoming regular after Clark gained an interest in Lilian, his childhood friend.

A well-known beauty of the school, Lilian was a star student, a top athlete and well known for her kindness.

But Aiden had a feeling Clark wasn't interested in any of that.

Like most of his targets, Clark was probably only interested in Lilian for her looks.

Her beauty put most women to shame and Clark was the kind of person Aiden refused to let Lilian get close to, even if he had to endure pain every day. That was his duty as her close friend. Even if he couldn't fight back, he could at least continue to deter a toxic, most likely abusive man from hurting her in any way.

"I've told her before, but she doesn't listen." Lied Aiden, his breathing still labored because now his shirt was strangling him.

"Well then, try harder. We've been at this for ages and yet here we are. How many times do I have to teach you the same lesson! Aren't you supposed to be smart?!" snarled Clark, as he punched the side of Aiden's head before throwing him at the floor.

His knees smacking onto the floor first, Aiden fell over and curled up into a ball as he held his legs.

Aiden didn't want to give Clark the satisfaction of hearing him scream, so he held back his tears and clenched his teeth while also bracing himself for the incoming kicking barrage he knew was coming. Which began moments later.

Aiden had thought, when it all began, that he'd eventually get used to the pain of being ferociously attacked, become numb to it and be able to shrug is off thus leading to his eventual triumphant turn around. But to this day, it still hurt just as bad.

"Let's go. I hear footsteps." Said Clark finally, after a few minutes had passed.

Kicking Aiden's scattered belongings away as he left, Clark randomly picked up a Hunter's book and threw it out a nearby open window, sending it spinning through the air and out of sight.

"Useless books for a useless thing," he spat as he left Aiden battered on the floor.

The sounds of Clark's footsteps receding along with his groupies, Aiden finally picked himself up using the nearby wall and put on his best smile while hobbling down the hallway.

Despite the fact pain was echoing throughout his body, he calmly gathered his things that were strewn everywhere across the floor and limped home feeling satisfied that while he had yet to win a battle against Clark, he was still one-sidedly winning the "war".

2

BEAUTY OF THE BEACH

Arriving at his home, Aiden put his hand on the scanner, which let out a soft beep as the "door" faded away, revealing a long hallway.

His personal school life aside, Aiden lived a fairly comfortable life thanks to the considerable wealth of his family due to the hard work his father put in daily.

"Is that you, Aiden?" came a voice from around the corner.

"Yeah, mom. How are you?"

"I'm doing fine, honey, how was school?"

"It was fine. Is dad home yet?"

"No, he's going to be coming home late today so we are going to have to eat without him."

"Alright."

"I'm worried he is overworking himself though. He's been coming home late for the last few weeks. I'll need to try and stay up, so when he gets home, he can at least be greeted with a warm meal."

"Don't forget to get enough sleep yourself, mom." Replied Aiden as he put his backpack into the closet in the hall.

"Don't worry about me, Honey. Oh! That reminds me, Lilian stopped by earlier, she said that her ESD broke and she really wanted to relax on the beach, so I let her use ours!"

"It broke? Didn't her family just get a newer model?"

"It seems the original installation guy made a mistake somewhere, so while she was scrolling through some of the options, it had a fatal error, and now it needs to be completely recalibrated. They will probably check the hardware for any issues too." Replied Aiden's mom, as she poked her head around the corner. "I also invited her to dinner."

An ESD or Environmental Simulation Device is a luxury item used to experience the joys of vacation without the crowds or traveling times. There was a lot of debate about whether it was a good product or a waste, but fans often argued that the device was excellent as a temporary fill-in for those times where you want just a few hours on the beach. A perfect device for satisfying the "Vacation itch".

"Be sure to say hi to Lilian before you go upstairs!"

Giving her a thumbs up, Aiden made his way towards the large room that made up the ESD and when he arrived, the interface screen showed that there was one inhabitant inside the room, experiencing the "Tropical beach" setting.

In response, Aiden tapped the watch on his wrist a few times and synced it to the room.

Once he did, he opened the door and, as he past the doorway, his outfit immediately transformed into one more fitting for the beach, which consisted of a pair of swim trunks, a pair of sunglasses and sandals.

A cheap yet effective set of clothes that did the job and wasn't terribly flashy.

Some design schematics could cost upwards of hundreds of dollars nowadays, especially those with unique programming for certain features or designs, but Aiden felt that things like that weren't necessary for clothes. After all, clothing was just clothing regardless of how it looked. As long as it covered what needed to be covered and served a function, it was fine.

Looking down the sandy beach, Aiden squinted his eyes as the simulated summer sun shone brightly into his eyes. This eventually prompted him to put on his sunglasses before walking towards the shore, which he figured was where Lilian was.

Trudging through the hot sand, Aiden continued looking around for his friend while listening for any splashing through the crashing of the waves until finally, he heard the slosh of someone wading through water or swimming.

Going through some tropical plants, eventually Aiden saw a small silhouette in the distance standing calmly, knee high in water, enjoying her time alone.

Gently splashing the water, the girl used her hand to block the sun from her face and Aiden took a moment to admire the beauty of the scene in front of him as he walked. Despite being surrounded by the pristine beauty of nature, the charm of the girl still managed to shine through, easily equaling if not surpassing the radiance of the artificial world around her.

By the time he got to the shore, his footsteps alerted the figure and she turned around.

Waving, Aiden took a seat in the sand as Lilian began wading in towards him until eventually, she was standing right in front of him, wearing a stylish, albeit revealing swimsuit that would have probably flustered Aiden if he wasn't so used to seeing Lilian.

"Hi, Lilian. Mom told me you were here so I stopped by to say hi. How are things?"

Scanning Aiden from top to bottom, Lilian let out a sigh and put her hand on her hip as she continued standing in front of him.

"I really wish you'd be more… stylish. You'd be so popular if you wore fashionable things."

"You mean, like you? With your goods bouncing around with just enough cloth to cover anything else?" replied Aiden with a smile.

"Leave me alone, I only wear this when I know no one else is watching. Sometimes I feel risqué, ok?"

"I'm watching…"

"You don't count. It doesn't bother me if it's you. You don't leer," she puffed.

"Cause I'm used to it." Aiden replied, with a nonchalant shrug.

"… Anyways, I'm doing ok. I'm sure your mom told you my ESD broke, right?"

"Yeah, that's a shame. It's the latest model, right?"

"Yeah, a repair drone is doing diagnostics now and it might not be fixed until tomorrow but I really wanted to just relax on the beach right now."

"Something bothering you?"

"Nothing more than the usual."

As an awkward silence fell over the pair, Aiden looked out toward the fake horizon until Lilian took a seat next to him and pulled her knees up to her chest.

"Dinner will probably be ready soon." Said Aiden.

"Fantastic. I am a bit hungry."

"When aren't you?!" laughed Aiden, his eyes drifting to Lilian who was watching the orange horizon which was programmed to be perpetually displaying a beautiful sunset.

"I can't help it! I love food! There is nothing wrong with loving food!" pouted Lilian. "Besides, it's not like I get fat."

"Not in your stomach at least." Muttered Aiden.

"Did you say something?" glared Lilian, her burning gaze piercing Aiden's neck as he smiled widely. "Wait, where did you get those?!"

Suddenly grabbing Aiden's arm, Lilian pointed to the new bruises Aiden had just gotten and looked at them with worry in her eyes.

"I was practicing some new anti-supernatural techniques; they didn't quite work out, but I'm sure next time they will."

"Gosh... Aiden, maybe you should stop doing that. Ever since you started doing that supernatural, paranormal stuff, you keep coming home with new injuries. Do you really love it so much that you are willing to hurt yourself in the process every day? Do you really care that much?"

Gently putting his arm down, Lilian frowned while crossing her own. Her eyes drifting to the rest of his new bruises and marks.

"Well, some people might call me crazy for it, but I think what I'm doing is worth getting hurt for every day. After all, it's very important to me."

Smiling weakly, Lilian let out an exasperated sigh as she shook her head disapprovingly.

"If you say so. I'm just letting you know though that if I start getting white hairs early, it's because of you."

"I'll keep that in mind." Aiden chuckled.

"Aiden!! Lilian!! Dinner!!"

His mother's voice echoed faintly from the next room and the duo looked at each other briefly before Lilian popped up and began quickly skipping towards the exit without waiting for Aiden. Who was literally left in her dust as sand flew up onto him and got into his mouth, causing him to start sputtering.

Right as the door opened, Lilian's clothes transformed into a pair of shorts and a white T-shirt as she entered the home and Aiden quickly ran over to catch up to her as she held the door open, the fire in her eyes telling him that while she was kind enough to wait, she didn't want to wait long.

"Ah, there you two are!!"

Greeting them with a smile was Aiden's mom who put an abnormally large pot of food down in front of them.

An aging woman with silky black hair, Aiden's mom was known for having a very naturally stern looking face but the kindest aura imaginable. Although woe be to the people that made her mad because, despite her small stature, she was definitely capable of being fierce.

"So, Lilian, I decided to make extra for you because I know how you like to eat, and a growing girl needs proper nutrients!"

"Yay! Thanks, Mrs. Elrod!!"

Lilian plopped down at the table, in her usual seat, as she bounced eagerly. The spot known as hers due to how much time she spent at Aiden's home since her parents were rarely ever home.

This in the past, led to Lilian being a very lonely, sad young teen but with the help of Aiden's mom, Amantha, she was quickly turned back around to being a cheerier person.

This was because more often than not, rather than having the young woman eat alone in her empty home, Amantha made sure to bring Lilian over any time she was willing to visit so she could experience some of the warmth of being able spend time with a family.

Her views being that a proper, happy and warm home environment was critical to healthy child development. Which seemed to be working out in Amantha's eyes as she watched Lilian grow into a wonderful young woman.

Piling food onto her plate without any regard for Aiden, who hadn't gotten any himself yet. Aiden's mom simply laughed as she continued constructing Lilian's mountain of food, but when Aiden began serving himself, he could feel his own mom's judging look as she measured how much he was eating.

"Don't eat too much Aiden, you've been looking a bit pudgy lately!"

Aiden rolled his eyes as his mom wiggled her eyebrows at him and began digging into his meal.

Despite his mom's typical commentary on his weight, she never really did much to limit his meals, which made Aiden feel like she was just doing it to bother him for the sake of poking fun at him. Although Aiden did feel like he had been neglecting his physical health lately.

Dinner lasted about thirty minutes and, without any real effort, Lilian had successfully cleaned out her plate, leaving nothing behind but a clean dish which didn't really surprise Aiden, who had barely managed to finish his own serving.

"Dessert?" asked Aiden's mom, as she saw Lilian twitching like she usually did when she was still hungry.

"I-if you don't mind."

"Of course not dear, something sweet to end a savory meal is a must!"

Getting up from her own plate and putting it in the dishwasher which spat out them out clean after only a few seconds, Amantha opened up the fridge and took out a freshly made cheesecake with glazed strawberries on top.

Immediately, Lilian's eyes lit up and Aiden could have sworn he saw stars in her eyes as she followed the cheesecake's movement intently from the fridge, all the way down to the table.

"O-only one slice, though." Said Lilian as Aiden's mom cut the cake.

But in the end, she ate three without any remorse, hesitation or guilt.

"Thanks, Mrs. Elrod! That was delicious!" hummed Lilian as she cleaned leftover cheesecake from her face.

"I'm just glad you liked it!"

Getting up from the table, Lilian immediately headed toward the washer and began feeding it dishes to start the cleaning process, while Aiden polished off his last few bites of cheesecake, which he had decided to eat against his better judgement.

Throwing in plates, utensils, and cups, Lilian happily did her work as Aiden's mom happily watched her while sipping a cup of hot tea that she had made before letting out a sigh.

"What's wrong, Mom?" asked Aiden, worried about her uncharacteristic sigh.

"It's nothing. Are you caught up with your schoolwork?"

"I have some homework to do actually." replied Aiden with a similar defeated sigh. "I've been slacking a bit, although I doubt I'll do any worse on the next test because of it."

"Oh! Actually, Aiden could you help me with some of the problems?" chimed in Lilian as she dried her hands and gently waved her head to fix her hair.

"Helping my rival, whose been aiming for my number three spot?" asked Aiden with playfully suspicious eyes.

"Uh… yeah? It's more of a challenge that way, don't you think? Or are you scared that if you help me, I'll surpass you without much trouble?"

"Highly unlikely," Aiden said as he rolled his eyes and, with a smile, he opened up his school-pad along with the homework folder.

Taking a seat next to him, Lilian brought out her own school-pad and Amantha watched the two with soft eyes before deciding to retire to a different room, silently leaving them to it as they became entranced in their school work with Lilian asking the occasional question and Aiden immediately answering.

3

CAT AND DOG

The next day, Aiden was alone in the club room when he heard a strong series of knocks on the door, which made him excited at the thought of having an interested soul visiting, but reality quickly caught up to him since no one ever really came to his club. At least no one that wasn't looking for trouble unless it was Lilian, but she was currently at tennis practice.

Standing up from his seat slowly, Aiden walked toward the door, and another set of powerful knocks echoed throughout the small room.

Then the doorknob jiggled and as Aiden grabbed it, the door slowly opened.

"Hello?"

Taking a step back, Aiden looked up to see a red haired, statuesque woman step in, her face stern but without any real animosity.

In her hand, she was holding a familiar looking book and, as Aiden turned his head to get a look at the cover, the girl suddenly handed it to him.

"I believe this belongs to you."

"Me?"

"You're Aiden from the paranormal research club, right?"

"Am I famous now? That's nice." Replied Aiden, as he took the book out of her hand.

"Well, as the one who goes around 'purifying' things, your name certainly gets around. Although I wouldn't use the word 'famous'."

"Well, all publicity is good publicity, right? At least it brings some awareness to something I think needs to be more carefully tended too."

Looking around the room, the girl walked past Aiden who placed the book on a nearby desk.

The girl carefully scanned Aiden's shelf which held all his paranormal related books. Which included a few of his special books which spoke of the legendary, mythical "Hunter" organization and a few random cookbooks.

Searching through the shelves, as if looking for something in particular, the girl picked out a unique book, one that Aiden personally considered a crown jewel in his collection because of its rarity and difficulty to find, but as the woman opened it, she looked through it with a certain familiarity, almost as if she already knew the book inside and out.

Impressed and drawn to her, Aiden slowly walked up behind her and by the time he had gotten to her side, she had already seemed to have found the page she was looking for and read what she wanted.

She then closed the book and replaced it on the shelf.

"Uh…"

"Where did you find these books?"

"I traveled a bit, the one you just read was the hardest to find. I like to stay informed. As a paranorm-y myself, I have to say you have good taste to be drawn to that one."

"I see… thanks."

"Are you perhaps interested in the paranormal? Would you like to join my club?" Asked Aiden eagerly, figuring this was probably his best chance to get a new member.

"I'm unfortunately already part of a club. But you wouldn't mind if I stopped by from time to time, would you?"

Tilting his head, Aiden ended up coming to the conclusion that she liked the paranormal like him, but her circumstances limited her ability to express that hobby, so with a smile, Aiden nodded his head rapidly.

"Fantastic. I'll be seeing you soon then."

Walking past Aiden, the woman left the room without saying anything else, leaving him alone and confused but also still excited about the idea of sharing his love of the paranormal with someone else.

* * *

Days passed and the young woman continued visiting on occasion like she said she would, opening the same book and flipping to different pages.

Eventually, Aiden asked for her name in a somewhat fearful manner and she told him her name was Rosalia, which was a name Aiden was used to hearing around the school.

Rosalia Lionheart was an athlete who was often referred to as "the star among stars." Her background was shrouded in mystery, having suddenly transferred into the school about a year ago and going on to take the school's female swim team by storm while also being unmatched by any other athlete in virtually any other sport.

No one knows why she settled for the swim team, but most didn't complain because as long as she was there, she couldn't take anymore "thrones" from other clubs.

After all, being the best gave you near total immunity to virtually anything, so by losing that throne, so too did the benefits disappear, regardless of how good you were.

The principal only cared about the very best and if the sport was team related, she maybe cared about the runners up.

"You wouldn't happen to have the third volume to this Codex, would you?" asked Rosalia one day, as she went through all of Aiden's shelves in the clubroom.

"Well, I actually do have it, but I don't keep it here. That one is very special so I keep it at home, but if you want to read it, I could bring it tomorrow?"

Scratching her chin, Rosalia thought for a moment before turning toward Aiden who was still getting used to her towering height and the subsequent, probably unintentional, intimidating aura that she exuded.

"Is it ok if I visit your home today?" she asked nonchalantly. "I'm in a bit of a hurry to read something in that book, it's only a specific thing I'm looking for but I don't want to inconvenience you too much by making you run home and come back."

Lifting the cup of tea in his hand to take a sip, Aiden read a few more words of his book before freezing, causing hot tea to spill over him.

"Ow! Hot!!"

Jumping up from his seat, Aiden dropped the rest of the tea and as he watched the liquid heading toward the book he was reading in slow motion, his heart dropped.

But before the liquid could destroy the pristine pages of the paranormal book, a swift hand snatched the piece of literature out of the air.

Despite still burning from the hot tea, Aiden stared at Rosalia in awe, totally amazed by her speed and reflexes, but before he could say anything, his brain forcefully reminded him that his important bits were under attack by steaming hot tea.

"Ooooow! Ah!! How did you do that!?"

In pain but still blown away by Rosalia's prowess, his curiosity drove him to ask a question despite his current state, and Rosalia simply shrugged in response.

"You should be more careful." Was all she said as she gently dusted the cover and placed the saved book back on the shelf where it came from.

"I know, I know. Your question caught me off guard…"

"Why? Do you believe I have some sort of different intention in mind? I just want to visit to look at the book quickly."

Narrowing her eyes and crossing her arms, Rosalia made one forceful sniff, causing Aiden to clear his throat.

"I-I know that."

"Well, do you mind then?"

"No, not at all."

Sitting back down in his chair, Aiden looked at Rosalia who nodded once before turning back to the shelf to sift through more pages.

* * *

"R-Rosalia…"

A tense atmosphere hung in the air in front of Aiden's home as Lilian stared at him and Rosalia blankly. Her pupils dilating a bit as a certain level of annoyance came over her features.

Having opened the door to Lilian casually dancing and singing in the hallway as she usually had the habit of doing, Aiden had expected her to be somewhat embarrassed at being caught playing around by someone other than him, but instead she seemed rather irritated as her aura of jubilance fell apart when she noticed the tall woman behind him.

"D-do you two know each other?" asked Aiden meekly, pointing between them as tension built up between them. Becoming almost tangible.

"Unfortunately." Replied Lilian as she shook her head gracefully and took on a very powerful, domineering pose with one hand on her hip that Aiden called her "Queen" stance.

"I didn't think I'd find the most popular and desired woman from our school in another, unrelated man's house." Started Rosalia as she crossed her arms. Unfazed by Lilian, who, despite being considerably shorter, was somehow matching her in overall aura of ferocity.

"That's none of your business." Returned Lilian, with a tone laced with so much animosity that even Aiden felt a chill go down his spine. He hadn't heard Lilian talk to someone like that in a long while, which made him wonder what their history was.

"That's true, although it makes me wonder how many other men's houses you are visiting."

Rosalia took a step forward and leaned in so close that she was almost touching foreheads with Lilian, who didn't back down a single centimeter. Forcing Aiden to jump in between them and put his hands up.

"R-Rosalia! You misunderstand, Lilian isn't that kind of girl!"

Giving the boy brave enough to get in her path an impressed but also skeptical look, Rosalia stood back up straight, with her fist on her hip as Aiden continued waving his hands while stumbling over his words in a manner she found cute but in a strange way.

"Then, are you two in a relationship?"

"No!" sputtered Aiden

"That's none of your business!" snarled Lilian at the same time, her eyes growing wide for a moment as she processed Aiden's answer and then gave him a quick glare afterwards.

Rosalia dropped her fist from her hip and scratched her head for a moment before letting out a sigh and looking away at the horizon for a moment.

"Regardless, I am here for a certain thing. Aiden, if you could bring it out. I'd prefer not to be too close to the snarling chihuahua there."

"R-right! You can come in if you want, though."

"No, that's o-"

The door slammed shut in Rosalia's face before she could finish as Lilian threw her full force behind closing it and the blond-haired girl spent no time pinning Aiden against a wall and thrusting her finger in his face afterwards.

"Why is she here? Why are you helping her!?" She demanded.

"B-because she seems interested in learning about the paranormal?" stuttered Aiden as he tried to free himself to no avail.

"Oooh, so you'll help any cute girl as long as they are into the paranormal? Hm?" raged Lilian as she started poking Aiden's forehead.

"This is unusual, even for you." Said Aiden as he watched Lilian's finger continue to go forward and back to poke him. "I know you sometimes have beef with people, but you've never let it out on me before."

"I…"

Her voice catching, Lilian suddenly took a step back and grabbed the hand she was poking Aiden with before placing it in front of her.

"Sorry… you're right. You don't know."

"You know how I feel about you carrying resentment and anger around, Lilian." Scolded Aiden, his own finger coming up and wagging at Lilian who looked down shamefully. "We'll talk about this later, and get all that negativity out. Maybe even make amends with her. But, whatever the reason, right now, it's poking my head, maybe later it gets worse if it festers. We need to fix it, now."

To anyone else, it would seem Aiden was being overdramatic or overly sensitive to such a harmless gesture, but no one else knew Lilian like he did.

Her getting physical with someone out of anger was a very rare thing. A dangerous thing as well, because in the past, she had hurt someone important to her because that person let a "harmless" gesture get out of hand.

"Sorry..."

Like a child, Lilian frowned and sniffed before walking down the hall, but after taking a few steps, Aiden came up behind and gave her a big hug, accompanied by a sigh.

This action helped cheer Lilian up as a small smile appeared on her face and she turned a little red. But, before Aiden could see it, she quickly escaped his embrace and disappeared into the kitchen, leaving Aiden feeling like maybe he'd just made her madder.

"No. I need to be stern." Aiden assured himself. "A good friend keeps their friends on the right and good path."

Nodding his head, Aiden finally got around to running upstairs, and by the time he got back down with the book and opened the door, he found Rosalia sitting on the floor, weaving some flowers together into a braid of sorts.

"You know, I'm impressed she set the door so she could slam it in my face. If it had simply appeared, it wouldn't have had the same effect."

Finishing one last twirl on the braid, Rosalia pocketed her creation and stood up.

"Why does she dislike you? Lilian usually isn't like that. Like… she really seems to be cross with you about something."

"You'd get a better answer from her, I'm sure. Even though we don't get along, Lilian doesn't strike me as a liar, so I'll leave it to her. I have things I need to attend to."

Taking the book with a thanks, Rosalia looked through the book quickly, finding a certain page that Aiden was shocked about, simply because it was somehow hidden between two other pages. A secret self-contained excerpt, 2 pages long, which was hidden perfectly between two specific pages that were half of the other pages' width.

"Wha…"

As she closed the book, Rosalia held it out and Aiden took it before being able to ask his question and before he could attempt again. Rosalia was already leaving.

"You want to stay for a drink or something? Maybe a snack?" Yelled Aiden.

"I'm OK. Besides, I doubt Lilian would appreciate me "intruding" in your home. Perhaps some other time and at some other place."

Raising her hand up and waving her goodbyes, even after she had turned the corner, Aiden could clearly see the top of

Rosalia's head over the large wall separating his home from the street.

Opening the book in an attempt to locate the "hidden" page again, Aiden had no luck finding it or any trace of its existence for that matter, which made him wonder how Rosalia knew about it.

"Oh well… there are people who know more than me in the world…" mumbled Aiden as he went back inside. "I should probably go talk to Lilian too." He finished with a sigh as he rubbed the back of his head.

Heading into the kitchen, Aiden went into the fridge and grabbed a large tub of ice cream along with a spoon before heading upstairs.

When his mom saw him, she simply nodded and backtracked into her room to continue watching T.V. already being privy to what was going to happen.

But, before he could make it up the stairs, a large crash startled Aiden, causing him to drop the ice cream and spoon before an explosion of dust and debris flew in his face.

4

MIRAGE OF VAMPIRE?

Blown back by the immense force, Aiden almost started tumbling down the stairs but was saved by the house's automated "fall" detection system, immediately catching him but freezing as its circuits broke from whatever was happening in the second floor.

"What's going on!?"

Running up the same stairs with a frying pan, Aiden's mom stopped as she caught a glimpse of her son and he responded with a shake of his head.

"I'll go up, Lilian's up there! Stay downstairs!" yelled Aiden as he made his way back up the stairs, his footing almost lost a second time as a powerful shockwave ripped through the house.

"Lilian!!"

Finally getting a good enough grip on the ground to run up the stairs, Aiden began calling Lilian's name as he rushed through the second floor but when he burst into her room, he came across a sight he wasn't expecting.

On the floor, over in the corner, laid Rosalia holding her side as Lilian stood with her hands gripping long, black arms.

Aiden couldn't identify what she was fighting, because it seemed to be wearing a black onesie, with all of its body hidden behind the cloth and on its head, it wore a helm which sported an expressionless, off-putting mask that had red painted cheeks.

"Lilian!"

Her face scrunched as she continued fighting for dominance with the intruder, eventually Lilian managed to somehow overpower it, twisting its hands back before pulling it down into her knee which she threw up at its face.

Her knee made solid contact and its face flew up but Lilian followed up with a fierce jumping roundhouse kick that sent the attacker flying into the wall, which cracked as the thing made contact with it.

"Who are you?!" yelled Lilian as she landed and massaged her now free hands.

But the intruder didn't speak. Instead, he simply got up without a word.

"R-run!" rasped Rosalia as she struggled to get up, blood dripping from her mouth, a sight that sent a wave of fear down Aiden's spine as he rushed over to help her while taking his shirt off to act as a bandage for her wound.

"Do you know who that is?" asked Aiden as he helped Rosalia hobble further from the being.

"It's not a who... it's an it!" coughed Rosalia. "And it's going to be much more powerful once the sun finishes setting..."

Aiden looked outside, through the new hole in the house wall and realized the sun was almost gone, preparing to leave everyone in darkness for the night, but while he was indifferent to it, the enemy who was still squaring off with Lilian, suddenly started laughing.

"Good... good..." it said, with a slight lisp before taking a powerful fist to the jaw.

Not many people were aware that Lilian knew how to fight, and the few that did, often learned the hard way.

In fact, Aiden figured he was probably the only one who had learned about her abilities peacefully, since he'd started self-defense classes with her.

Although he was never very good at it.

Lilian on the other hand seemed to be gifted in the martial arts as she took to it almost immediately. It was almost like her body knew what it needed to do. As if her instincts were already hyper honed, but despite her instructors' desire to have her pursue martial arts further then just learning self-defense, Lilian had stopped actively going to classes after learning enough to protect herself.

Which still made her fairly unstoppable.

But, as the sun set, Aiden saw for the first time, his childhood friend lose ground to an assailant.

Like a bolt of lightning, the second the sun was gone, the man disappeared and within a moment had landed a powerful, violent blow against Lilian, sending her flying back despite having managed to block the punch with her crossed arms.

"Ah, the night is so much better." Said the man, as he turned his head inhumanly far to the side, before turning it back to face forward with a sharp crack.

His outfit then dissolved into a black mist before reforming into the shape of a well-crafted black suit.

That was when, for the first time, Aiden saw the intruder for what he truly was.

"Vampire… "

The mask over his face now gone, Aiden saw the monster sported sharp fangs, sunken eyes, and an ugly wrinkled visage. But, these qualities didn't last long as the Vampire rejuvenated in front of Aiden's eyes into a dapper young man who could have easily been a model. A sickening sense of dread washing over him as the creature returned to its prime.

His eyes had become sharp and handsome while his hair now appeared smoother, slicked back and as dark as the deepest black and as he looked at Lilian, he flashed her a toothy, sinister fanged smile.

"How lucky." Was all he said as he took a step forward, but he suddenly stopped and took a step back with a hiss.

Looking at the floor, Aiden noticed a small line of salt right in front of the Vampire, which had spilled out of a slightly torn brown pouch on the floor that Aiden had never seen before.

"Tch."

Stepping around the feeble line, the vampire regained his smirk but Aiden, who had been paralyzed with fear and shock, suddenly felt a sharp jab in his shoulder.

"Use this!"

Dropping a silver cross necklace in his hand, Rosalia stood herself up and brought out what seemed to be a handle of sorts which sprung to life and extended into a full-fledged blade as she flicked her wrist.

"You study the paranormal, right?" asked Rosalia as she took a step forward. "My Light blade can hurt him, but he's too fast for me to hit without damaging his spirit first."

"Damage his spirit?"

"Salt, silver, crosses, garlic. You know. The usual. I need you to get close enough to actually touch him. I'll take care of the rest."

Shaking, Aiden watched as the Vampire looked menacingly at Rosalia before scoffing and picking up Lilian.

"Ah, this wretched smell. How I've waited to do this."

Licking his lips, the vampire opened its mouth wide as it prepared to bite into Lilian's neck and despite her frantic struggling and kicking, she couldn't break the grip it had on her.

"That won't work on me anymore, sweetie. To you, my body is like stone."

Baring his fangs to her flesh again, Lilian's eyes went wide as the teeth neared her neck but before he closed his mouth around her, the Vampire let out a fierce roar as the sizzle of something burning erupted from his side.

Driven to action by the thought of Lilian getting hurt, Aiden discarded his fear while baring his teeth. He gathered up his courage and charged forward in two long strides, successfully jamming the cross necklace Rosalia gave him into the vampire.

There was a moment of triumph that washed over Aiden as he listened to the Vampire yell, but it didn't last long as he was swatted aside and ended up slamming into the wall in the far distance.

Aiden felt his ribcage crack from the Vampires wide sweep but as he spat out blood, with murder in his eyes, he jumped back into the fray and put the necklace over the monsters' neck before pulling down with all his weight.

The silver digging into the abomination's flesh, the vampire was forced to drop Lilian and fell to one knee as it clawed at the silver beads.

"Insolent human!!" roared the Vampire as he grabbed the beads despite them burning his hands. "It will take more than a random silver object to defeat me!"

Bucking backwards, the vampire sent force straight into Aiden's stomach, further cracking his ribs and at the same time slammed the young man into a wall as he evaded Rosalia's sword strike.

"I'm not that weakened that I won't see such a slow attack coming, fool!" he sneered as he began jabbing his elbow into Aiden.

But Aiden didn't let go and, as he saw the unconscious Lilian on the floor, his body demanded revenge which dulled his sense of pain even further.

"You know, food tastes better when it's properly seasoned!!" yelled Aiden, as he yanked the vampire onto the floor with a surprise pull.

"Gak!"

Thrown off balance, the monsters' face was slammed into the ground and as he made contact, a more explosive sizzle came from his face which prompted him to begin screaming.

On the floor laid the scattered remains of the brown pouch's contents, which were multiple layers of salt that Aiden noticed at the last moment.

Smiling victoriously, Aiden's strength faltered for a moment which led to him being violently thrown back toward the wall as the Vampire ripped off the cross necklace from around his neck.

"I'll drain you like the cow you are first!" roared the Vampire as he grabbed Aiden, who had blacked out from his head hitting the wall first.

The Vampire held the side of his face with his teeth bared but just as began opening his mouth to sink his teeth into Aiden, his eyes went wide and blood spilled out of his mouth.

Taking the opportunity to land the decisive strike, Rosalia swung her sword and sliced through the supernatural creature like butter. It's blade glowing a brilliant red as the Vampire screamed in defiance.

Now cut in two halves, the Vampire fell back into the random patches of salt, further burning him. But at that point, the pain from the salt was nothing compared to the burning that crept its way up his body.

A cut from a properly made light blade was extremely painful simply as a scratch to many paranormal monsters, but to be fully sliced in half, the pain alone was often nearly impossible to survive.

Even for a creature like a vampire that boasted extremely high regenerative skills.

So, slowly but surely the glowing red ring that formed the cross-section of Rosalia's swing continued spreading, turning more and more of his body into dust until finally, his last hair follicle turned to ash.

Breathing heavily, Rosalia drove her blade into the ground for support as she continued holding the wound on her abdomen.

Aiden's shirt was now sopping wet with blood and Rosalia shook her head in disappointment at being caught off guard, but looked at her two fallen classmates with interest, especially Aiden.

Before giving it much thought though, Rosalia took out a thick needle, then jabbed it into her wound which sent a surge of pain so vicious through her body that her vision flared red, but by the time it passed, she was well enough to quickly gather the Vampires remains and jump out of the hole that was made when she was thrown into the house.

Then, as she left, Rosalia threw a drone toward the house which deployed a holographic field showing the building completely repaired and on its own it began fixing all the damage. Which included tending to injuries and carrying out the proper procedure for victims caught in the "net".

* * *

"D-did we win?"

Getting up, Aiden rubbed his head and, as his brain remembered the events that had transpired, he started waiting for his body to begin hurting but when the pain failed to register, he began looking over himself in confusion.

Checking his arms, pants, shirt and just about anywhere else he could reach, Aiden was shocked to find himself completely fine without any sort of injury or scratch. In fact, he was even in his pajama's which struck him as odd, until he realized what time it was.

"Was... that a dream?"

Shaking his head, Aiden put his arm down and realized he was laying on the bed in the guest room, but as his arm grazed something warm, he looked down and became even more confused.

Laying in the bed next to him was Lilian.

Softly breathing, she was unharmed in any way but what Aiden was slow to realize was the kind of outfit she was wearing.

Letting out a short snort, Aiden covered his mouth and looked around a few times before checking to make sure he had pants on so he could safely jump out of bed.

"That's pretty... exotic." Whispered Aiden as his eyes fell back onto Lilian.

Wearing very risqué clothes, Lilian had a lingerie set that consisted of a semi-transparent top which somewhat covered but barely contained her overflowing assets and extended down to her hips.

And it didn't take a genius to tell that she probably only had underwear on and no real bottom with her outfit, but that realization aside, Aiden was trying to figure out how they'd ended up in this situation.

In his mind, he had just fought a Vampire with Rosalia, who there wasn't a single trace of.

"Did I imagine it all?" asked Aiden to himself as he thought about the possibility that perhaps he came up with the ice cream, caught Lilian sleeping, and for some reason decided to sleep next to her and dreamt the whole frightening event.

"The ice cream!"

Looking around, Aiden looked for the dessert which he remembered he dropped before coming upstairs, but right there, on the far desk, the confectionary treat was waiting, slightly damp from melting, with the spoon he had grabbed for Lilian.

Aiden felt nothing but disbelief as he was forced to accept the circumstances and amid his own self-denial, Lilian let out a small groan before smacking her lips and turning toward him. Wrapping her arms around his waist while making an upset face until she snuggled closer to him.

Scared, because Aiden knew that if Lilian woke up right now, she'd freak out, the trapped man looked for a way to escape but couldn't see any.

It didn't help that Lilian was also pressing her body more and more into his as the seconds passed, but eventually, after about thirty minutes, she turned back over to the other side, giving Aiden his chance to bolt.

Not wanting to spare a single second, Aiden jumped out of bed and ran straight into his room where he plopped into his bed, his mind already logging his encounter with the "vampire" as a dream and nothing more. His brain power being more preoccupied with the events he knew were real such as Lilian in her mind-blowingly sexy outfit. A fact he would never repeat to anyone, even himself.

"When did her taste get so mature in sleepwear?" was the last thing Aiden said to himself before falling asleep, a subtle fear in his heart about doing so due to the desire to not dream about Lilian getting hurt again.

5

CHOCOLATE HUNT

The next morning, Aiden had gone up to his mom to ask about the day before but she said that all she remembered was a red-haired girl coming by, Lilian getting angry and Aiden going upstairs with ice cream.

She had no memory of any sort of explosion, destruction or "battle" with any supernatural entities. A fact that made Aiden's mom look at him with a small, affectionate smile as if she were talking to a small child recounting an imaginary battle.

Regardless though, he couldn't accept it. Even Lilian was confused when she woke up about why she fell asleep in their guest room and despite having changed into her normal clothes by the time Aiden saw her again in the morning, he couldn't help but get a bit flustered as they made eye contact.

A fact that immediately tipped her off that he had seen her "mature sleepwear" which immediately caused her to burn a bright red before storming away.

"I only wear that kind of stuff because it's comfortable, OK!? I get hot at night easily and the thin fabric helps keep

57

me cool!!" she yelled as she stormed out of the house while hiding her face. "I'm not that kind of girl!"

The door re-appearing in its frame, Aiden yelled out, "I thought you looked good in it!" down the hall in a last-ditch effort to make her feel better, but when she yelled back "Shut up!!", he knew it hadn't worked.

In hindsight, Aiden, after some thinking realized it probably would have been better to say that sort of stuff was normal or something along those lines. After all, there was likely no doubt in Lilian's mind that she looked good in it. It was probably the fact that she thought it was indecent that bothered her the most.

"I guess I'll need to bring her some chocolates later… " said Aiden to himself.

Lilian's favorite candy was chocolate from a very specific chocolatier, which, while not terribly expensive, was fairly hard to get one's hands on because of the chocolatier making limited amounts of chocolates per day in order to preserve the highest level of quality.

Still, if there was one way to turn a possibly bad situation around with her, it would be to give her that chocolate. Although it wasn't a foolproof plan as other men had figured out this weakness of hers to try and abuse, only to be met with tragic failure.

"Just need to talk to Bertrand."

Picking up his school bag, Aiden quickly put on his shoes and ran out the door after saying his goodbyes to his mother, eager to get to the chocolatier's store.

There was a young man there named Bertrand who was that chocolatier's grandson. He and Aiden had gotten to know each other after they both took a beating when Aiden attempted to save him from bullies. Through that shared experience, a friendship had blossomed despite them being fairly different people.

Because of that though, Aiden had a reliable way to gain access to the sought-after chocolates, which was something not even Lilian knew about and was something he hoped to keep a secret from her because he knew that otherwise, she'd pester him to the ends of the earth for a constant supply.

* * *

"Oh? Aiden? It's been a while."

Leaning over the counter, a young man about Aiden's age with long black hair pulled back in a ponytail, gave him a smile.

He was wearing a black shirt, long jeans and a white apron that was stained with chocolate. Which was an optional addition and obviously for decoration since most fabrics were self-cleaning nowadays.

And while it was somewhat unnecessary, it definitely helped to add a sense of authenticity to the small, but popular shop.

"Hey Bertrand. Do you think you can give me the usual?"

"A pack of six of our Doppio Choco Supremes? I should be able to, but it's a good thing you came early today… " finished Bertrand as a solemn look came over his face.

"Why?"

"Gramps isn't feeling so good lately. A few days ago, he just became really ill and even though we've had doctors look at him, they've all said they don't know exactly what's wrong with him… they've just prescribed some over the counter medicine but, I haven't seen it help much."

"Maybe he's overworked?"

"I thought so too, but I don't think that's the case." Replied Bertrand, as he shook his head slowly." Gramps isn't the first to fall ill like this. As if overnight, a lot of people have started showing the same symptoms."

"A pandemic?" asked Aiden, as his eyes went wide.

"Maybe, it'd have to be a really fast spreading one though… anyways, I'll go get the chocolates, but you should be careful. If it is a disease, it could be spreading even now. It could also be nothing, but I'd rather over prepare then under prepare. You know?"

"No, I totally get it. I'll keep an eye out, and I'll tell Lilian. Since she tends to worry about things like that." Finished Aiden with a small frown.

Nodding once, Bertrand went to the back of the shop, and moments later, he returned with a small, beautifully crafted box.

"Try not to upset Lilian too much, alright? Until Gramps gets better, supplies are limited. I'm not as fast or as good as Gramps yet so… yeah."

"This is his batch, though, right?" asked Aiden as he gently opened the box and put a handwritten note he had made beforehand inside.

"Yeah… what, you don't want chocolates by me?" questioned Bertrand as he narrowed his eyes.

"Pft, nah, I'd rather have your Gramps batch."

"Tch… ah! Get out of here, Aiden."

Bertrand made a "shoo"-ing motion with his hand as Aiden began swiping his card and he let out a laugh as the purchase went through. Then suddenly, Aiden felt a chilling gaze on him from somewhere to his side, causing him to immediately tense up.

"What's wrong?" asked Bertrand with a confused expression.

Turning toward the source, Aiden saw nothing in the store except the displays and the shadows, but even as he looked at the wall, he could have sworn that there was now something looking back at him from the other side.

"N-nothing. I'm sure Lilian will really like these, thanks again man."

"Anytime, Bro! Just be on the lookout and stay safe!"

Giving Bertrand a thumbs up, Aiden left the shop and, when he entered the sunlight, almost immediately, the foreboding glare on him disappeared as if warded off by the light.

"If it isn't Aiden."

Standing in front of the store window with her arms behind her back, Rosalia was carefully inspecting the structure of the chocolate shop when she noticed Aiden walk out with some chocolates.

"A fan?" she asked, as Aiden walked up to her.

"A bit. I take it you're waiting for the store to open? Buying some yourself?"

"Something like that." She stated flatly, as her eyes traced the building's layout.

"I didn't think you'd be into sweets, since you seem to be so into fitness."

"Only things in excess are bad for the body. The occasional indulgence in sweets helps keep morale up, and the sugar can be useful. But, yes, you're right, I am not usually one to partake in something like chocolate."

Her manner of speaking strangely more formal and articulate, Aiden furrowed his brow and chanced a question that he had been wanting to ask her.

"Hey, do you remember... and this might sound crazy... fighting a Vampire?"

Rosalia's body freezing, she turned to face Aiden with a suspicious look.

"No. Why? Do you?"

"Uh... er... Kinda... " replied Aiden while rubbing the side of his arm.

"Interesting."

As Rosalia's attention turned back towards the building, Aiden saw her take out a notebook and jot something down. It was an old-fashioned way of keeping notes, but still effective especially since it was pretty easy to take out and reference.

"I'll be waiting for the shop." Said Rosalia suddenly. "No point in you waiting for me. While I do appreciate you letting me look at your books, I wouldn't necessarily call us friends. Thus, you have no obligation to wait for me."

"T-that's fair." Replied Aiden, slightly crestfallen. "I'll be on my way then. Good luck."

"Thank you."

Leaving Rosalia to continue her "inspection" of the chocolate store, Aiden made sure to put his fresh chocolates in his bag where they could remain cool so that he wouldn't deliver melted chocolates.

Lilian loved chocolates but really hated melted ones. One time, Aiden made the mistake of not watching their temperature and he received an extremely lengthy lecture on the importance of making sure chocolates were delivered in a pristine state, otherwise, it was insulting to both the maker, the receiver and the deliverer.

"The highest form of disrespect to everyone involved" as she so blatantly put it.

But that didn't stop her from eating them. Instead, she just ended up complaining about the lost beauty and flavor profile of the "defiled" treats.

So, with some pep in his step, Aiden jogged his way to the school, hoping to run into Lilian somewhere along the way or, failing that, meet up with her secretly in the school, since he wasn't in the mood to incur a certain hot-heads wrath.

But things rarely every worked out so well for the young man, which was why as soon as he set foot on the other side of the gate, a heavy arm snatched him to the side and Aiden found himself being thrown against the backside of a nearby building.

"Hey there, Aiden. Old buddy old pal!"

Gripping Aiden's shoulder fiercely, Clark was giving him a big, intimidating smile as his goons grabbed Aiden's bag and dumped the contents.

"I heard an interesting rumor that there is a certain chocolate that Lilian is very partial too... and a birdie told me that you just so happened to have picked up some of those very chocolates today! You weren't planning on giving them to her, were you?"

Clark was tightening his grip on Aiden's shoulder as he spoke and as the chocolates from his bag hit the ground, Aiden could almost feel Clark's increased animosity come off of him.

"I bought them for myself... "

"Oh, really? Well, then I suppose you won't mind if I take them and give them as a gift to Lilian, do you? You know, as my friend, do me a solid?"

Clark roughly picked up the box and Aiden could feel the urge to yell "No" at him as he began shaking the contents, probably damaging the carefully crafted insides with his aggressive movements.

"Hm. I'll never get that girl's obsession with these, but if there is one thing I've learned, it's that girls really will do anything for their favorite foods. It took me a while to find Lilian's favorite, but now that I know it and you so conveniently delivered it to me, I suppose it'll be smooth sailing from here on!"

Laughing to himself, Clark let go of Aiden and began walking away, but in a bid to get the chocolates and run, Aiden lunged for Clark's hand.

"Huh?"

Easily dodging Aiden, Clark lifted his arm causing Aiden's fingers to just barely miss their mark.

Falling to the ground without any reward for his effort, Aiden looked up and Clark smiled sinisterly before kicking Aiden's jaw, knocking him out cold in a single, brutal move.

6

THE SWEET TRUTH

His eyes fluttering open, Aiden let out a sharp gasp as he tried to open his mouth only for a shot of pain to radiate up his jaw muscle.

Scratching at it, he realized that there was gauze wrapped around his jaw completely, stopping right below his mouth.

"Ow…"

"Aiden!"

From the side of the bed, Lilian spoke up as she realized that Aiden was finally waking up after being asleep for a few hours, her heart jumping the moment she saw him turn toward her.

"Lilian… how are you?" asked Aiden awkwardly, the restrictions on his mouth reducing his speaking ability.

"I was so worried about you!" cried Lilian as she wrapped her arms around him, hugging him tightly.

"It's alright, I'm ok… how'd you know I was here?"

"Well, it's the strangest thing. I was in class and Clark came in, complaining how he was almost late because he had to help the "paranormal guy" by taking him to the nurse. Obviously, I asked why and when he saw that I was sad, he gave me his box of Chocolates! He said he stopped by early to get them, but felt like it seemed like I needed them more! Seems like he's a pretty nice guy after all."

"yeah..." muttered Aiden.

"Anyways, as soon as I heard, I came over here and I've been waiting for you to wake up!"

"What about class? You shouldn't be missing class for my sake."

"It's fine, I got the teachers permission. So, do you want to eat some of the chocolates?"

"Well, they were given to you and they are your favorites so... "

"I don't mind one bit! I'll gladly share my chocolates with you, but I want to know how you ended up hurting yourself... was it another one of your "paranormal experiments"?" asked Lilian as she took the box of chocolates out and set it on her lap.

"Yeah... sorry. And I just said I would stop being so reckless." Laughed Aiden.

"Gosh... what am I going to do with you?"

Chuckling softly, Lilian opened the lid of the chocolates and she furrowed her brow as she realized the contents had a note on the inside. At first, she assumed it was some sort of love letter or invitation to go out which Lilian wasn't interested in accepting, but as she took it out, she noticed the hand-writing was familiar.

Then, as she opened the note, her eyes went wide in shock.

"Clark didn't buy these chocolates... " whispered Lilian as she stood up, causing all of the treats to fall on the floor. An action that Aiden only noticed as Lilian's shadow cast over him.

Aiden's eyes drifted over to Lilian's hand, where he noticed the note he had put inside the box originally and almost immediately he felt his body tense up.

Why had he tried so hard to keep Clark's actions hidden from Lilian? Was it because he didn't want her to worry? Or was it because Aiden was scared that she would take care of the problem much more efficiently than he could? Was there something he wanted to prove to himself and the bullies or was he simply afraid of looking weak and pathetic to Lilian? Not even Aiden knew himself, but he knew that with the note now in Lilian's hand, there was no purpose to his charade any longer.

"Aiden... " said Lilian, rage creeping into her voice as her eyes slowly turned toward him. "I-is... are all these times you've come home hurt... have you been lying to me? These "dangerous Paranormal experiments" ... are they just a cover up... because things like this were happening?"

"I-I don't know what you're talking about." Replied Aiden, instinctively trying to continue hiding the truth.

"Don't lie to me! This is your handwriting and your name on the bottom! Why would Clark give me chocolates that he said were for him, and there be a note from you inside?!"

Crunching the note in her hand, Lilian gripped the table fiercely as she turned toward the door.

"Lilian wait!" yelled Aiden as he grabbed her wrist. "It's not worth it!"

"Not worth it?! After all the times I've seen you come home so badly hurt!? Maybe it isn't worth it to you, but do you know how much it hurt me to see you so beat up every time?! I always brushed it aside because you told me it was you pursuing your passion, so it can't be helped, but now I learn that the truth was you were being attacked… bullied by someone! How do you expect me not to do anything!!"

Grabbing Lilian's wrist with both arms, Aiden felt himself be pulled out of the bed almost effortlessly by the enraged Lilian, but as she noticed him about to fall, she immediately helped him back on his bed before taking a reluctant seat in her chair.

"Tch. Scum. Waste of space. Dead meat." Growled Lilian as she crossed her arms. "So, why did he do it?"

"How do you know he was bullying me? Maybe… "

"Quit lying to me, Aiden! We supposed to always tell the truth no matter what to each other and you want to lie to me about something that's hurting you!? How am I supposed to trust you!?" yelled Lilian as she slammed her hand on the bed.

"Sorry... he started doing it because he hated how close I was with you... he wanted me out of the picture so that he could... take you... "

"Huh!? For such a dumb reason... he... "

"It's ok. Really. Now that you know... well, I don't know what will happen but... you know."

"No, I don't know." replied Lilian angrily, but after a few more seconds, she let out a sigh and put her hand on Aiden's head. "But... knowing you, I bet you did it for me... in your own weird way."

"..."

"Thanks."

Giving Aiden a warm smile, the fire in Lilian's eyes almost immediately vanished and it seemed like she had regained control over her emotions, which ended up leading to Lilian giving Aiden another long embrace.

"You suffered for my sake. Like an idiot because you didn't need to... but still... "

Lifting his arms to return the embrace, Aiden thought about how Clark was going to react when he realized that Lilian knew about the bullying.

He wasn't going to be happy, that was for sure, but the real question was about how he was going to react or how he would retaliate, if at all. That was what worried Aiden the most, because while things could get more painful for him, he was more worried about Clark taking a more forceful approach with Lilian.

Lilian and Aiden ended up spending a lot more time in the nurse's office, talking about and going over everything Aiden had gone through. Each new bit of information making Lilian angry but in a controlled way that she was able to hide fairly well.

Eventually, Aiden finished his "report" and, with a long sigh, Lilian simply shook her head before picking up the chocolates on the floor and throwing them away.

"I'll forgive you for this, if you can get me a new box tomorrow." Said Lilian as she walked back from the trash can. "I'm sure you have your reasons, but that doesn't mean I have to be happy about being lied to. Especially when it comes to something like this."

"I suppose that's fair." Replied Aiden, who was starting to feel bad about lying the whole time.

"But! In exchange, since I know you were doing your best to look out for me, I'll do something special for you."

"What?"

"You'll have to wait and see!" said Lilian with a wink.

* * *

Days passed and Lilian, upon request from Aiden, was still withholding the fact she knew about Aiden being bullied from Clark.

Since their time in the nurse's office, Lilian had started being very attentive and aware of his whereabouts at all times. Most likely in an effort to keep him safe, catch Clark red-handed, and be able to unleash her currently contained wrath before Aiden could get hurt.

Which, while appreciated. Made Aiden feel bad about himself. Like a weakling who needed others to keep himself safe.

This led to Aiden resolving himself to start exercising. So that he could strengthen himself so he would never get bullied again or be too weak to defend himself or those he cared about.

And it was with this resolve that Aiden found himself at the doors to a local gym which had just gotten a membership to.

Frankly, he didn't have any real experience in the art of working out, but Aiden figured that it couldn't be too hard. After all, to him, it was just lifting heavy thing. It couldn't possibly be too difficult to do.

But, as soon as he entered, he was almost immediately proven wrong as he was overwhelmed by the countless different machines that were all constructed differently, with all kinds of different shapes and colors. Immediately knocking the air out of his sails.

"Let's go with dumbbells."

Deciding to stick with the basics after being intimidated away from everything else, Aiden attempted to confidently walk over to the dumbbell rack but ended up instead getting in almost everyone's way who was using free weights, except for a few who were against a wall.

That was when he noticed a familiar face, glistening with sweat, doing dumbbell curls while carefully controlling her breathing.

Stopping mid-step, Aiden was entranced by Rosalia who was currently in the middle of her workout. She looked similar to an Amazonian warrior, her body well defined and toned, strong and beautiful.

But at the same time, even while awestruck, Aiden felt fear creep up on him due to her imposing height. Which, despite his immediate impression of undeniable beauty, was augmented by the very athletic build he was admiring.

Noticing Aiden, Rosalia looked over to the out of place looking boy but continued doing her set as he walked up to her.

"What brings you here, bookworm of the paranormal?" Said Rosalia, in between repetitions. Her form flawless.

"Bookworm? Well, I guess it's true. Uh… well, I… wanted to start working out and I decided to come, but… "

"But you're lost?" finished Rosalia as she put down the dumbbells on the ground, softly.

"Yeah… "

Aiden looked down and rubbed the back of his head, but looked up when he felt a hand on his shoulder.

"No reason to feel ashamed. It is admirable that you took the first step to come here, now you just need to learn."

"But how?"

"If you like, I can teach you. Think of it as thanks for letting me read your books. I'm sure with a bit of work, you could become quite the formidable man as well."

Rolling her neck, Rosalia began walking away while rotating her shoulders.

"Today won't do though. If you come tomorrow in the morning, I'll be able to help you. Right now, I'm almost done with my circuit. Although, if you really want to get started today, I'd recommend some light cardio. Running, perhaps, or swimming if you prefer that."

"Are you sure I won't be a bother?"

"I happen to enjoy teaching those willing to learn, and it's not like you'll slow me down. We will be working at my pace, so while it'll be quite hellish for you, I think it'll benefit you in the end regardless."

Aiden gulped as Rosalia sat down at another contraption and began doing seated bicep curls.

"Of course, that's just an offer." She finished, her face showing signs of strain but also, somehow, maintaining her air of calmness.

"N-no, I'd be honored... I mean... I'd really appreciate it."

"Great. Oh, and tomorrow is leg day."

"Uh, does that mean what I think it does?"

"You'll see." Chuckled Rosalia. "I'll see you tomorrow then."

Giving Aiden a final nod, Rosalia continued her set as he walked off toward the running simulator.

Punching in a terrain to simulate, Aiden felt the plastic ground turn into soft grass beneath him and he began gently joggling through a fresh, well cut pasture. The action almost immediately tiring him out and making him dread of what tomorrow would bring in regards to Rosalia's workout regime.

7

SURPRISE RETALIATION

"Lift, Aiden! Lift!! It's only two more!!"

His face going red from exerting himself, his veins feeling like they were about to burst and with his legs having long been enwrapped in burning pain, Aiden struggled to do his ninth and tenth squat.

"Don't let that bar defeat you!! Go!!"

Becoming unusually passionate, Rosalia was standing behind Aiden as he struggled to lift just the bar on his second set.

An embarrassing fact and one he wasn't aware of, since he could have sworn that he was at least strong enough to add some weight to the metal rod. Which was a mistake that cost him dearly earlier on his first set, but was now rectified.

"Graaa!!!"

Letting out a long groan, Aiden finally managed to lift the bar up and, as it reached its apex, his legs gave out and he fell over with Rosalia holding the bar and gently placing it back on the rack.

"Ow... ow... ow... "

His legs throbbing, feeling nauseous and hating himself, Aiden laid on the floor until Rosalia effortlessly picked him up and plopped him on a nearby seat.

"That wasn't too bad." She said with a small nod. "If you keep putting in hard work like that, you'll be squatting like me in no time."

Her voice, while usually monotone and matter-of-fact, now had a kind tone to it and in her eyes, a small sparkle glimmered as if for the first time in a while, she was having fun.

"Thanks… do people usually like leg day?"

"I wouldn't call it a fan favorite, it has some zealous followers though. Some men like to skip it, and they end up with toothpick legs. Not something I'd recommend." Answered Rosalia as she started putting forty-five-pound plates on the squat bar.

"I can see why… " joked Aiden. "How much are you putting on there?"

"I'm starting at a healthy two-hundred and twenty-five pounds, then I'm going to max out on my last set with three-hundred."

Aiden's eyes going wide, he watched as Rosalia finished putting the weights on, the bar itself starting to seem like it couldn't handle the weight, and as she chalked her hands, she quickly clapped them together before going under and taking a deep breath.

"Alright."

Rosalia's eyes sharpening, she lifted the bar with a small grunt and took two steps back before going down and slowly coming back up.

"One." She whispered to herself.

Repeating the motion over and over again, Aiden couldn't find the words to describe what he was seeing and, after ten repetitions, she put the bar back on the rack as she let out a final, long, hissing breath.

"Wow, you're amazing." Said Aiden absentmindedly.

"Thanks. Although, I think I can go further, but it seems like I've hit a certain wall."

"You want to lift more?" said Aiden, shocked at how ambitious she was while also wondering if it was even humanly possible to go higher.

"Always." Was all she said as she shook each leg out, preparing for her next set.

There was a certain beauty in the sheer determination she exhibited.

Here was what many would consider the peak of physical fitness, an athlete who had reached the maximum but rather then be satisfied, she contained pushing her limits every day without rest. Sporting a hunger to improve that left Aiden speechless.

Aiden couldn't imagine what drove her to such lengths, but as he watched her battered, sweating, barely able to walk, he couldn't help but develop a deep admiration for her.

Sure, Aiden was in a similar state, but how could he compare himself to her?

* * *

A few hours later, Aiden had showered and was in school on the way to his clubroom. His mind was still filled with awe and a newfound respect for Rosalia.

"I was wondering what was taking you so long. Been hitting the gym? Hm?"

Passing a corner right next to his clubroom, Aiden tensed up as he heard Clark behind him and, as he turned around, he found himself suddenly pushed against the wall with a firm hand gripping the collar of his shirt.

"Thanks for the chocolates, Aiden." Sneered Clark, his lackeys coming up behind him. "Ever since I gave them to Lilian, I've noticed she's been watching me from time to time. I guess in the end, she really is just like any other girl. Give her something she likes and she'll spread her legs."

Clark's comment hit a certain nerve in Aiden and his face turned into a scowl while he grabbed Clark's wrist.

"Take that back!"

Aiden tried to release Clark's grip but considering he was fresh out of exercising, the gap in strength between them was even worse than usual.

But, despite knowing that, Aiden tried harder than usual to fight back and the reason why was simple. He wasn't going to let him talk bad about Lilian or treat her like some sort of object that exists just to please him..

"Oh? Has your time in the gym put some more pep in your step? Given you some baseless confidence that makes you think that you have some sort of better chance against me!?"

Clark let out a snort and thrust his knee into Aiden's leg, causing him to yell as an unfamiliar pain shot through his body, his sore muscles screaming at the sudden external aggression.

"Well, would you look at that. You can yell." Leered Clark. "How nice."

"You don't get to say stuff like that about Lilian!" snarled Aiden, still struggling with Clark's fingers. "You don't deserve her! You only see her for her body and nothing else, you'll never understand how nice she can be, how goofy, ditzy, how unique she is! I'll die before I let someone like you get close to her!"

Suddenly releasing Aiden, who fell onto the floor writhing, Clark readied another kick with a scowl but before he could deliver his attack, a hand suddenly appeared from behind him, gripped his throat and threw him into the wall.

"Gah!!"

Crashing into the hard surface with enough force to send a loud thud throughout the hall and rattle his teeth, Clark quickly shook his head before focusing his eyes on his assailant. His expression looking as if he couldn't believe anyone would raise a hand against him.

"How shameful, Clark."

"R-Rosalia…"

Standing in her school uniform, her hair still drying, but with an undeniable authority and overwhelming aura, Rosalia looked at Aiden, who was still on the floor and took a step toward Clark, who had to fight the urge to flinch.

His two goons had been knocked unconscious by Rosalia, who'd swiftly and silently slammed their heads together before going for Clark and the bully was now left undefended in a situation where he, for once, would have to fight fair and square.

"Rosalia, just walk away. I know people, I-I can end your career here. You're just a transfer student!"

Grabbing Clark by the throat and lifting him into the air, her previous fatigue seemingly gone, Rosalia looked Clark in the eye, making him seem exponentially smaller with each passing second until he seemed miniature compared to Rosalia.

"You think you can pull that on me, of all people?" calmly stated Rosalia. "How about this. You leave the boy alone. You never get near him again and I allow you to keep your ability to play sports."

Her voice like ice with no compassion, Rosalia continued staring at Clark as he began to struggle against her grip until finally, he decided to take his chances and throw a kick at her face.

In response, Rosalia simply stopped it with her free hand and in a single fluid motion, quickly jabbed his hip with the same hand.

The moment the blow made contact, Clark's eyes went wide with pain but before he had the chance to scream from his now fractured hip, Rosalia jabbed his throat, preventing any sort of sound from escaping by crushing his trachea.

"Ok, how about this... you leave him alone, and I won't do the same to the other side."

By now, Aiden had recovered enough to look at the scene unraveling from the floor and as he stood up he could see tears begin to form in Clark's eyes as he began nodding his head.

"Good."

Dropping him onto the floor, Aiden could see the pain in Clark's face as he tried to catch himself but inelegantly fail as he fell over due to his now fractured hip.

"You won't get away with this!" coughed Clark through clenched teeth. "You'll regret this, I guarantee it!"

Unimpressed with his threat, Rosalia put her foot on the base of Clark's neck and began applying pressure, forcing his head into the ground.

"I don't think I caught that correctly. I think what you meant to say is that, in return for me letting you continue to play sports, you will leave Aiden alone and never speak of this again, or else you may tragically lose function in both legs."

"Screw you!"

Shifting from her foot to her knee, Rosalia readied her fist to deliver another swift punch, but as she began pulling back, Clark's tone suddenly changed.

"W-w-wait! Wait! I'm sorry! OK? OK?!"

Clark squealed as Rosalia's fist flew down, but she ended up stopping mere centimeters short and got up.

"Scram, and take those two with you."

"I can't, I don't even know if I can walk!"

"Figure it out."

Grabbing his two lackeys by their collars, Clark began hobbling down the hallway and looked back at Aiden for a moment before turning forward as Rosalia glared at him.

Once he was finally gone, Rosalia let out a long sigh and shook her head.

"You can come out now."

Confused, Aiden began scanning the hallway until Lilian popped out of the corner with a meek look.

"H-hey, Aiden."

"She gave me a quick rundown of what's been happening to you." Explained Rosalia. "She also said I could be as rough as I wanted with him as long as he got the message. But what I don't understand is why she didn't do it herself."

"Because if I did it, I'd probably murder him." Admitted Lilian as she crossed her arms with a low growl. "Anyways... thanks for helping."

"I don't mind. Never liked him anyways."

Lilian put a hand on her hip and looked away from Rosalia who simply sighed and gently helped Aiden walk into the classroom, one of his legs now less functional than the other.

"She's a good person." Said Rosalia, as they entered the room. "A bit stubborn, but anyone who is willing to swallow their pride for a friend isn't all bad. At least not to me."

"Yeah. She's something." Chuckled Aiden. Sitting down in his usual chair.

"Y-your quite something yourself." Replied Lilian, her eyes meeting Aiden's as she walked into the room. "When you stood up to Clark to defend me... that was something... "

Her cheeks turning red while twirling her hair, Lilian looked at Aiden quickly and spared a glance at Rosalia before turning on her heels.

"I owe you one... Rosalia."

"If you say so."

Strutting away, Lilian left the room without another word. Her own mind processing the series of events and the words of Aiden when he stood up for her.

She always knew that Aiden babied her and was protective of her, but she never imagined he felt so strongly about her. At least not to the level that she just saw.

That made Lilian happy, feeling that Aiden truly respected her and valued her. Two things she already knew but, for some reason, the affirmation of those facts made her bubble with joy.

8

HELLHOUND

"You can't hide from me. I know you're somewhere in there."

Peeking into a random hole located on the school grounds, Aiden, with a flashlight on his head, was carefully looking for concrete proof of the mythical "gnome".

Lately, students had been having their belongings go missing and it was up to Aiden to find the true culprit.

Sure, everyone else blamed a normal thief, but Aiden knew better. After all, he had seen one of them make off with a candy bar of his not too long ago.

Which was unusual because Gnome's were usually very slippery, stealthy and generally just hard to see.

So, now he was searching all the holes he could find throughout the school in order to uncover the true thieves and prove to everyone that he wasn't crazy.

"Ow. Nothing."

Shaking his hand quickly, Aiden watched as an angry rabbit made angry rabbit noises at him for intruding in on its home. It's fluffy white fur somewhat puffed out as it "lectured" him until it finally wiggled back in, kicking dirt at him before disappearing into the darkness.

"Onto the next one."

Picking up the jars, traps and other necessary equipment he would need to catch a gnome, Aiden stopped as he noticed Clark walking down the sidewalk, but as they made eye contact, Clark simply looked away as he gently rested his hand over his hip.

Ever since the incident with Rosalia, that was what their "relationship" had turned into. A welcome change in Aiden's eyes which was the icing on the cake since he later heard that Lilian went off on him in the middle of the hallway, ruining his reputation or at the very least damaging it, since in a battle of "whose word is worth taking", Lilian's was much more respected, valued, and trusted than Clark's.

"Hey, so. Is this a gnome?"

Holding a caterpillar in a jar, Lilian showed the container to Aiden who simply shook his head.

"That's... just a caterpillar, Lilian. Remember, I said gnomes are green..."

"Like this is."

"Yeah, but gnomes also have little hats and look like really tiny people."

"Right... "

Still worried that Clark would come after Aiden despite the threats and warnings, Lilian ended up quitting the tennis club and joining Aiden's paranormal Research Club in order to keep a closer eye on him.

Despite having managed to bring Rosalia to help him before, Lilian still felt extremely guilty about letting Aiden get hurt at all during the exchange. So, she ended up taking steps so that no matter what, except for in classes, she'd be right by his side at all times.

That didn't mean she suddenly gained an interest or even an understanding of the paranormal though, but as Aiden watched her shuffle through the grass on her knees, he couldn't help but smile because she was trying her best.

And that alone meant a lot to him.

"Is this paranormal?" asked Lilian, as she picked up a piece of wood, which at first Aiden thought was just wood. But when she turned it, he noticed a familiar symbol on it.

"This... this isn't "paranormal" per say but... it might be related."

Taking the piece of wood, Aiden shuffled through his bag and took out a book called "Hunters Codex: Guide for Combatting the Darkness".

Inside its pages there was a glossary of "symbols" and "runes" which were used by the mythical organization to combat the nastier paranormal abominations that appeared.

And, while Aiden had tried to mimic them for his own use, they'd never worked. No matter what he did, and there was nothing in any of the books that were related to or talked about the Hunters that defined why.

"This is a barrier rune. Used to ward off paranormal entities in a radius... it can be combined with other runes to form a large barrier or even as a containment field... according to this book." Said Aiden as he read the entry. "But... this is wood, and it looks pretty fresh. No way this could be ancient... could it be that... "

"What's happening here?"

Turning toward the familiar voice, Aiden came face to face with Rosalia who was hovering over his shoulder, her eyes locked on the piece of wood in his hands.

"Oh! Rosalia!"

"Oh... Rosalia... " said Lilian and Aiden at the same time.

"Look what I found! It's a rune used by the Hunters to ward off evil entities! It's on wood and it doesn't even look that old, maybe, just maybe, there's a Hunter whose been protecting us in secret!" said Aiden eagerly, as he waved the wood in front of Rosalia who swiped it out of his hands with a raised eyebrow.

"Perhaps. Or it could be that someone is pulling a prank on you. The Hunters disappeared a long time ago after all, and even if they still existed, what are the odds they would be here? In such a small city?"

"Well, I mean... yeah. I guess you're right."

Taking the piece of wood back from Rosalia, Aiden looked at it one more time in disappointment before putting it in his bag.

"Fake or not, It's a cool find. First time I've run into one of these and it's all thanks to Lilian! I don't know how I missed it!"

"Yeah, I don't know how she didn't miss something so small…" added Rosalia with an unusual edge to her voice, while looking at Lilian who was now sitting with her legs to one side. Waiting.

"What can I say. I have wonderful eyesight. Feel free to praise me as much as you like." She said while smiling.

"Right. Eyesight." Finished Rosalia. "Well, have fun with your paranormal search. Do you think you'll be back in the clubroom later? There is another book in there I want to look at."

"Oh! Yeah, but here."

Rummaging in his pocket, Aiden took out a keycard and tossed it up to Rosalia who quickly snatched it out of the air.

"That's the key to the clubroom, instead of waiting for me, I figured it'd be easier if you let yourself in." continued Aiden with a smile.

"You're… giving this to me?" asked Rosalia, as she turned it over in her hand, obviously puzzled. "This is a very important key, I don't think I've done enough for you to trust me so much."

"You seem interested in the paranormal like me and frankly, you done a lot for me. More than enough for me to trust you with something as small as the key to my supply closet club room."

"Aiden! Why are you giving her a key! What about my key!!"

Lilian used her arms to bring herself next to Aiden, a teary-eyed puppy dog look in her eyes, as she quivered her bottom lip.

"Why would you need a key?" asked Aiden, as he used his index finger to push her back by the forehead. "You'll only go in there when I'm there... right?"

"But Aiden!!" whined Lilian.

"What a strange sight. I suppose even the dignified, noble, and proud Lilian becomes a spoiled girl in the face of certain special people." Said Rosalia, a glint of amusement in her eyes which irritated Lilian.

"Ah, that's right." Said Lilian. "Is that a problem?"

Becoming suddenly serious, Lilian stood up and crossed her arms before standing face to face with Rosalia, but after a few seconds, she plopped back down next to Aiden.

"Er... Lilian?" asked Aiden, confused by what he just saw.

"Anyways. I'll be heading to class. You two can continue enjoying yourselves. Have a nice day, Aiden. Lilian. Thanks for the key, I'll be sure to keep it safe."

Putting her hands in her pocket, Rosalia walked off with a nod and left the duo to continue their search for the elusive gnome, but as Rosalia left Aiden's field of view, he spared one more look at the piece of wood and, as he traced the rune with his finger, which seemed too carefully made for a joke, it suddenly began glowing.

"What?!"

Shocked at the marking suddenly coming to life, Aiden dropped it to the ground and at the same time, Lilian jumped to her feet as she looked past Aiden down the end of the large schoolyard.

"What... is that?" she said as she pointed forward with a shaking finger.

Turning his head, Aiden's blood went cold before he could even set eyes on whatever it was Lilian was looking at and he heard a loud, echoing bark which, while similar to a dog, felt far more sinister, dark, and foreboding.

"It couldn't be... "

Upon meeting the source of the bark, Aiden's eyes went wide as a large, black dog stalked towards them, draped in what seemed to be shadows that dissipated into the air, its eyes glowing a sinister red.

"That's... a hellhound."

9

HUNTER

The loud bark echoed throughout the open courtyard and Aiden covered his ears as his legs suddenly grew weak.

Then, a thump forced Aiden to turn back around where he noticed that Lilian had fallen over.

"Lilian!"

Dropping down and carefully picking her up, Aiden put his ear near her mouth and was relieved when he heard the gentle, calm sound of her breathing.

"The legends are true... " whispered Aiden as he turned to look at the large dog that was edging closer and closer to them. It's posture communicating its position as a predator and vicious entity.

"Hellhound" was a term used to identify a certain mythological creature which was often described as a large black hound. Known as a harbinger of death, a sign of the ending of life, its abilities include a bark that allows it to make the unprepared fall into unconsciousness.

"Why am I still... "

Aiden's eyes suddenly shining in realization, he looked down at the cross around his neck that was hidden under his cloths.

It had been a gift from his grandmother that had most likely unintentionally just saved his life, but as the Hound became aware of the duo under the tree, Aiden's confidence in its abilities to protect him from the beast's wrath started to falter.

Lunging forward, the Hellhound turned into a trail of shadows that flowed through the air toward Aiden. The shapeless body of black wisps somehow feeling malicious and bloodthirsty despite having no true, solid form.

In response, Aiden tried to move Lilian but had only managed to tug her about a foot before the hound neared and he was forced to put his arms up in front of Lilian, a look of fear on his face but a determined conviction in his eyes as he began yelling, waiting for the creature's attack strike him.

Suddenly, as the beast opened its mouth after regaining its form, it stopped as if it had hit a solid brick wall right in front of Aiden. The Hound's body plastering into it completely before a surge of electricity went through it, sending it flying back.

"What?"

Looking at the floor, Aiden's eyes fell on the glowing piece of wood which was now shining even more brightly, causing the materials edges to begin blackening.

"It's real." Whispered Aiden.

"It's real!!" He repeated as he picked it up with a yell.

"Tch. I knew I smelled a Hunterrrr… " growled the Hound while shaking it's head. "But the scent is not yours… it's not exactly hers either… "

Circling the pair, the Hound growled as it kept an eye on the piece of wood, the blackened edges creeping closer to the rune on it, while crumbling away at the same time.

"Hmmm… "

Letting out a growl that somehow sounded as if it was thinking aggressively, the Hound vanished into black smoke again and suddenly attacked Aiden from the opposite side, its' speed at a level that he couldn't even properly react to, but once again the barrier held.

Yet, with each thud on the barrier, the blackening jumped a few centimeters until finally, the burning piece of wood was almost eating into the rune itself. An event that was shown by the light around Aiden starting to falter and crack.

"AWWOOOOOOO!!!"

Suddenly, the beast let out another fierce howl and this time, Aiden could feel his mind slip into unconsciousness, his legs turning to jelly rapidly.

"No!"

Grabbing the cross on his neck, Aiden felt the effects greatly lessen until he could finally keep his eyes on the Hellhound again.

"Heh. A cross. For not being a Hunter, you are quite well prepared… although all I smell on you is admiration. So, you must be a fanboy." It jeered, its face somehow adopting a mocking smile while it once again began circling them.

Suddenly, the Hellhound's ears perked up and it "phased" backwards just as a large sword cleaved the spot where it was previously standing.

CRASH

The ground exploded as the blade went through it which forced Aiden to cover his eyes from all the dirt and debris now flying through the air.

"what the… "

A surge of wind knocking Aiden off his feet and onto the floor, he struggled to open his eyes as the air became filled with more and more dust.

Swinging quickly, Rosalia lifted her blade as she spun to launch another attack at the Hellhound in front of her.

The Hound in response used a combination of dodges and phases to avoid the edge of the blade, but as it quickly learned, despite being wisps, the blade was capable of igniting and destroying pieces of it which forced it to rely solely on dodging.

What it wasn't expecting though was for Rosalia's empty hand to suddenly produce a large shield that she used to ram into it, sending it sprawling across the floor.

"Hunter!!!" it snarled, as it dug its claws into the dirt to hold its ground.

Not saying a word, Rosalia placed her shield in front of herself and steadied her sword on top, leveled directly at the Hellhound.

She waited for the creature's next move as she stood her ground, mindful of making sure that Aiden and Lilian were being properly covered.

Rosalia wanted to tell them to run, but a Hellhound's speed was greater than her own, so the further they got from her, the greater the danger they were in. Which meant their safest place was inside the almost broken barrier that she had placed a while ago, which was removed by an unknown force from its proper place before being found by Lilian.

And while normally, that'd be a huge annoyance to Rosalia, in this case, the fragment ended up saving the pairs' lives, which was something she could happily accept. Even if the broken barrier was the reason the Hellhound had made it into the school in the first place.

Taking a deep breath, Rosalia strengthened her grip on the blade handle, slowly sidestepping to match the Hellhound's circling until finally it lunged forward, splitting into two shadows.

Rosalia slammed one down with her shield while swinging at the other, causing the real Hellhound to dash back to its original distance.

"How well trained for an organization that hasn't been active for centuries." Spat the creature, while shaking out its fur.

The two engaged and disengaged multiple times, Aiden could feel his own mind starting to fade as the Hellhound occasionally barked, but to his surprise, Rosalia seemed to be completely immune to its effects. Instead, she was actually speeding up and becoming more aggressive with each short exchange.

"There has to be something I can do." Muttered Aiden as he started looking through his bag.

Grabbing a book, Aiden went to the "runes" page and quickly began reading through each of the symbols until he found the one he was looking for.

"Rune of spectral binding."

Quickly drawing the symbol to the best of his ability on a piece of paper, Aiden realized he had no way to reliably get it under the Hellhound. Making his efforts useless.

But that was when he noticed Rosalia drop her shield and produce a piece of paper of her own.

Barely dodging one of the Hellhound's claws, Rosalia took a step back and landed a kick into the dog's side before wiping off the blood on her face with the piece of paper.

"Spectral binding!!"

Throwing the paper directly under the airborne hellhound, it exploded into flames before tendrils of fire lashed out to restrain the beast.

In response, the Hellhound tried to evade the fire but was eventually grabbed and forced onto the ground.

"Accursed Elementals!!"

Unable to phase anymore, the beast began biting and thrashing, writhing desperately to remove the restraints but as Rosalia lunged with her blade, ready to decapitate it, it reared its head before letting out a fierce roar while bellowing out a torrent of flame.

Caught off guard, Rosalia dug her feet into the ground and put up her shield which split the beam of flames in all directions, scorching the ground, plants and even the air around her as a odd burnt scent that Aiden couldn't identify wafted into his nose.

Suddenly, the air around Rosalia shifted as three more Hellhounds appeared out of the air, each one snarling and lunging at Rosalia, who was still blocking the bellows of fire from the first beast.

Their jaws closing in on Rosalia, a small explosion of white dust around her startled all of the hounds, who jump back while letting out a sharp series of whimpers and at the same time, the first Hound ran out of energy to continue its fiery assault.

"Salt?"

Tasting the air, Rosalia looked back as she dropped her shield and saw Aiden in a throwing position, with a second bag of salt in his other hand, ready to throw.

Pleasantly surprised, Rosalia smiled and gave him a nod as thanks for the support before lunging forward to dispatch the immobilized Hellhound before it could recover.

But Aiden's actions acted as a double-edged blade because now, the other three hounds had their eyes set on him and as he quickly began making a salt circle, he could hear the barrier cracking as the three new enemies began ramming into it, the piece of wood ending up as ashes just as Aiden completed the circle.

"Salt is an ineffective barrier. Human. It is merely an annoyance. Nothing more." Growled one of the Hounds as it stood just outside of the salt.

"Then come get me." Challenged Aiden, fully aware that salt was probably not going to hold them back for long, if at all.

In response to his challenge, the three hounds looked at each other and seemingly sneered before opening their mouths to let out one unified bark.

The bark of one Hellhound was enough to make Aiden feel uneasy, despite having a cross around his neck but with three happening at the same time, Aiden simply blacked out. His brain turning off like a computer that was unplugged the wall socket.

"Sit."

His vision fading to black, Aiden's last few moments of consciousness were filled with a scene that seemed to be straight out of an apocalyptic movie scene as spears of fire cascaded down from the sky. Piercing every Hellhound mercilessly.

Putting an immediate end to the long, heated battle.

10

THE LEGEND REALITY

"In a small town? Why would… "

"I don't know. The one in charge of the registry never did his job, so we don't have any records."

"It was Leroy, wasn't it?"

"Yes. We thought he could, but… well anyways. The point is we've gotten lucky and found two more. For better or for worse."

"I think this is the first Retainer we've found."

"Aye, we don't have many sleeping either."

"Which makes any Retainer that much more important."

Standing over the sleeping body of Aiden and Lilian, a pair of masked individuals held a discussion that no one else could hear. Their voices holding a certain hollow, almost mechanical tone to them.

Wearing gloves, boots, long cloaks and a hood, these two people showed no skin, and their motions were at times very stiff. Only distinguishable from each other by their cloaks, with one being accented with blue and the other with red.

"Hm. It's funny how these two were found together, don't you think?"

"It is, Dominal and Ezkiel were great friends."

"Not just that, their families had been friends for generations before those two. We always joked about those two families being "together forever", but I never thought it'd be so true."

The two men chuckled to themselves, and one of them brought their arm up, revealing a golden badge of a wolf on his breast.

"I still can't get used to this though." Said the man, as he rotated his shoulder, a subtle creak coming from his joint.

"Not like we have much of a choice. The beacon was lit, and as planned; we answered. Although I agree the circumstances were less than agreeable. Things could have been better."

"I blame Jenkins."

"Well, it's our fault for entrusting two fairly important things to two of the more...dubious members of the time."

Shaking his head slowly, the man in the blue cloak brought his hand up to his mask and made a pinching motion as if to grab the bridge of his nose, but as his finger touched nothing, he stopped.

"Oh, right."

"Anyways, we will let the church take care of them and we will brief them after they've fully recovered."

"There's potential here. Hellhounds are troublesome creatures, especially when in a pack. So, to survive with no training at all, that is quite impressive."

"Diluted or not, Dominal and Ezkiel's excellence still leaks through, I suppose." Laughed the one in the red.

"Means they are one of the few worth bringing in and truly training. Hunter Rosalia did well."

"But she is still inexperienced. In time though, her true skill as a descendant of the Scarletguard family will shine. Luckily we had Hunter Sophia to provide backup."

"This time. We sent Hunter Rosalia to a small city so she could hone herself in relative safety. With all the hot spots appearing, even we are currently overwhelmed. But for there to be so much activity in this small place, we might be missing something."

"We need to reevaluate. I agree that there might be something we are missing, or it could be that the Phantasms know better than we do where our descendants lie… "

"And perhaps they are hunting them down before we can find them."

"Exactly."

"Then we need to start being more proactive and aggressive. Even if things are a bit harder now than before."

Nodding to each other, the duo began walking towards the exit when it opened and a small violet-haired woman wearing the clothes of a nun entered.

Giving the two large men who towered over her a smile, she carefully maneuvered around them with the large platter she was holding that contained two separate plates of food.

Sitting down next to Aiden and Lilian, the nun placed the food to one side before gently cleaning her hands, taking a bible out of a holster on her hip and opening it while the two men simply stared.

A few seconds passed in silence, after which the duo eventually exited the room, but as the door closed behind them, the one in blue made a strange sound as if he was trying to smack his lips together and the one in red sniffed.

"It wasn't just me, right?" asked the one in blue.

"No, no I felt it too."

"I've fought all manner of beasts and monsters, but that… " said the one in blue as he pointed at the door. "… That frightens me."

"I suppose the church is still the church."

Nodding his head in agreement, the one in red motioned for his friend to start walking and together they left the building with long, somewhat awkward steps.

* * *

Hours would pass until Aiden woke up, the two mysterious men having long since left and the nun at his bedside diligently and without any exhaustion, continuing to read her book as she waited for all her patients to open their eyes.

It was a mundane task but one she felt was highly rewarding for, in her eyes, she was doing the duty asked of her by her Lord. She was making the will of her deity a reality and that was all she needed to continue onward without hesitation.

So, when it came to the time that Aiden would finally open his eyes, the Nun simply put her book away gently and greeted him with a warm smile as a confused look spread across his face.

"Where am I?" he asked, as he propped himself up on the bed.

"Hello. You are currently resting in the nursing ward of the Church of Saint Stolus."

"Why am I in an Ignati church?"

"You will get all the answers you need in due time. For now, eat."

Turning softly, the nun opened the small door of a temperature control box and took out one of two plates which looked just as fresh as it did when it was made hours ago.

"I was... fighting Hellhounds and the... Rosalia... "

Rubbing his head to unscramble his brain, Aiden felt a gentle finger on his forehead which stopped his train of thought and as he looked up, he saw the smiling violet-haired nun give him a spoonful of what looked to be meat and potatoes.

"Please, eat." She said.

Taking the bite of food, Aiden slowly chewed it and he began looking around the ward.

On initial observation, the ward appeared to be very old. Using torches for light and being constructed of what seemed to be pure brick. The medical bed that Aiden found himself laying on somehow seeming to be the most advanced item in the whole space despite the fact it was just a simple mattress.

Suddenly, Aiden felt a soft poke at his side and he turned his head to see Lilian groaning until her eyes finally opened a moment later.

Almost immediately, Lilian sprung up and seemingly out of reflex let out a wild haymaker that knocked Aiden out of the bed and onto the Nun who let out a squeal as the food spilled over the both of them.

The punch hitting Aiden right under his ribcage, he tried to get up but when the object of support that he was using ended up being suspiciously soft and tied to a soft squeal, Aiden quickly threw his weight to the side and laid on the floor on his back.

"Lilian… you need to fix that habit." Muttered Aiden, as he stared at the ceiling.

"S-sorry… " replied Lilian, as she poked her head up from over the bed, an apologetic smile on her face.

Reaching down, Lilian helped Aiden get back up and, as he stood up, he looked over to where he thought the nun was going to be but was surprised to find just the foodstuff all over the ground.

"Where did… "

Looking around, Aiden realized the nun was now on Lilian's side, her clothes dirty from the food but a warm smile still on her face.

"I'm so glad that you've awaken. You seem very healthy and energetic." She said with closed eyes.

"Sorry… I… if I wake up in a place I don't know, my body just… it's like a defense mechanism and… "

"No, no. Please do not worry about it. Women must always be ready to protect themselves. The world can be a dangerous place after all." She replied. "I applaud you for training yourself so well."

Lilian chuckled nervously and looked at Aiden for answers, who gave her a thumbs up, which made her immediately relax.

"Apparently, we are in an Ignati Church, in their medical ward." Said Aiden.

"Ignati? The guys who worship the fire and sun?"

"Not quite, but I suppose to those who do not study our faith in-depth, that's what it may look like." Chimed in the nun.

"What are we doing here?"

"Well, actually, I am supposed to send you somewhere once you two have awakened! There is a certain group of people who wish to speak with you!"

Clapping her hands together, the nun then reached into her pocket and brought out a small notebook which she flipped open and, after spending a few second reading it while nodding to herself, she looked back at the confused duo.

"Follow me!"

Happily marching toward the door, Aiden looked at Lilian and then at the disregarded second plate of food before getting in line behind the nun with Lilian almost hugging him from behind with how close she was.

"We will be transporting you to a new location. Unfortunately, there are a few things that need to be put in order at *their* medical wards. So, we were asked to help nurse your wounds this time around. We were happy to oblige though, since we've always worked together since time unrecorded!"

"Right… "

Guiding the duo through a series of corridors, doors and hallways, eventually they reached a large door which led them outside to a floating car that seemed normal, except for a strange glow that Aiden noted but couldn't quite identify.

"That will take you to where you need to go."

Bowing, the nun closed the door behind herself and left Aiden along with Lilian outside, weary and unsure whether they should enter the car until Rosalia came out of the passenger seat, wearing a strange but elegant uniform.

"Come on then." She ordered.

"Where are we going?"

"To meet the Hunters."

11

OMEGA COUNCIL

The car the duo rode in had rendered itself invisible as soon as they had entered and as they sat down in the well-crafted seats, Aiden noticed that the windows in the back were completely blacked-out. Making it impossible for him to see outside as the car made its way down the road.

A fact that left Lilian feeling uncomfortable and Aiden suspicious about the whole situation.

But, once they reached their destination, as Aiden helped Lilian out of the car, he noticed the car had a miniature wolf as a hood ornament along with a matching emblem that he recognized from his books. The discovery making him feel slightly better about everything and significantly more excited.

"Come on."

Urging them forward, Rosalia lead them through a large gate which had two warrior statues presiding over them and as they entered the estate, a long, overgrown garden greeted them which housed a cornucopia of different plants.

Although, as they neared the main building, the garden became much cleaner and neater. Telling Aiden that recently, someone had started doing proper maintenance on the grounds.

Eventually, Rosalia led them through the door of the large mansion-like building at the center of the grounds, but the interior shifted drastically as Aiden passed the doorway, giving him a strong wave of vertigo before he found himself standing in front of nine statues.

"Woah... "

Each statue seemed to have been made in the visage of a specific person and while it seemed like they were meant to be part of the same organization, they all wore different uniforms which, with a close inspection, could be interpreted as variations of the outfit which Aiden had seen Rosalia use to fight the Hellhound.

"Those are the Eternal Watchers."

A voice echoing from behind one of the statues, an inhumanly tall man wearing a red-accented cloak walked out of the shadows toward the center of the room and was followed by another in a blue-accented cloak.

"You stare at them so intensely, it's as if you can feel their awe-inspiring power despite them having died thousands of years ago."

Aiden turned toward the two figures who walked with a soft step, but whose upper body seemingly bobbed with each step and was at a loss for words.

Sitting square over their left shoulder, was a golden emblem shining brilliantly with a sheen that almost made it seem like it was glowing. The eyes of the wolf in the symbol seemingly glowing majestically like twin yellow topaz gems.

Rosalia had told him that they were going to meet the "Hunters," but Aiden had remained skeptical of that claim. They were a secret organization after all and while he had come up with hundreds of reasons to remain dubious about it, when the two masked men stopped in front of him, he couldn't remember a single one.

Instead, Aiden only felt excitement well up within him along with a child-like giddiness that threatened to overtake him as he looked up at the nine-foot behemoths in front of him.

"I feel this boy is more of a fanboy then a warrior capable of fathoming the grandness of the people immortalized in front of him. Which is unusual considering there shouldn't be any records about our organization."

"Unless… "

"… he wouldn't."

"Leeroy did say he enjoyed writing… "

The two looked at each other for a moment before eventually returning their attention to the awestruck boy in front of them.

"That's for another day… anyways. Allow me to introduce myself. My name is Arias, Grey wolf of the Hunters."

"And I am Serx. Also, Grey wolf of the Hunters. As Grey wolves, we are… "

"Hunters who achieved excellence in the field, veterans and accomplished ones at that, who chose to leave the front lines to teach new generations of Hunters!" blurted Aiden, getting a raised eyebrow from Lilian who had positioned herself behind him and was holding onto his shirt.

"I'm going to kill Leeroy."

"He's already dead Arias." Muttered the one in the red accented cloak.

"I'll find his grave, dig it up, drag his soul from the afterlife and on my blood, I'll kill him again."

"Not ethical, Arias."

Patting his friend on the shoulder, Serx shook his head and Aiden began doing mini squats quickly as his excitement continued rapidly growing.

"Yes, you are right. Later, we'd like to know where you learned that, but for now we have more pressing things to take care of, so please follow us."

"On my blood, Serx. On my blood!!"

"Arias, with so many things "on your blood" I'm surprised it still flows."

"Well, it doesn't technically."

"Fair."

Laughing together, the duo looked back briefly before clearing their throats.

"A bit of information that you may or may not know." Started Serx. "Those statues you saw just now. Each one immortalizes a great Hero from Hunter history. Warriors who were not just the greatest, most powerful Hunters of their eras, but also Hunters who accomplished unfathomable, impossible things. Earning them a spot as an Eternal Watcher."

"Wait, one second!" interrupted Aiden. "A... are you guys the real deal? Real modern Hunters?"

Serx and Arias looked at each other and, with a quick nod, stopped before taking off their hoods, revealing their full "masks" but also something Aiden wasn't expecting.

Metal.

"We aren't "modern Hunters". We are two of the Hunters who helped defeat and seal the four dark Avatars and cleansed the earth of darkness."

Taking off their masks, the duo's faces were those of robots. Not a trace of anything organic on any part of them, which shocked Aiden and made Lilian squirm in discomfort for a moment.

"We had hoped to awaken with our proper bodies but a... mishap forced us to use these backups."

"Yeah. "Mishap." Let's call it that. When in reality, the mishap was the one who did their job wrong." Muttered Arias.

"Anyways. We are part of a special group of Hunters that chose to be placed in suspended animation. So that we could be awakened should one of the Avatars ever be released."

"While not all Hunters ended up like us, some of us did and we are more or less unfit for battle without our full abilities. Which is fine for us since we were already grey wolves but some of our stronger warriors have been forced into the role despite having a real lust for battle."

"But not all, some are still pretty effective with just their weapons."

"True."

"Abilities?" asked Aiden.

"What, did the book not spill the beans on that?"

"N... no?"

"Hunters have more than just advanced weaponry and sigils to battle the paranormal. Hunters usually have a unique ability due to their bloodline that lets them do things like throw fire... or yell really loud in Siren's case." Finished Serx with a laugh.

"Siren would kill you if she found out you were still making fun of her ability after all this time."

"Yeah... "

A solemn smile somehow playing on Serx's static face and joy filled what should be lifeless, inanimate eyes, but he quickly shook his head and put his hand on top of his metal dome.

"Anyways. We are going to be doing your skills assessment shortly."

"Uh... what?" asked Lilian and Aiden at the same time.

"Skills assessment! Your performance against the Hell-hounds, based on the report we got, was sufficient enough for us to consider you for the Hunter's organization. Plus, you are both direct descendants of former Hunter families."

"We... what?" said the duo at the same time again.

"Oh, don't worry, I'm sure you will both do fine."

"And if you don't, well at least you'll be healed before we erase your memory." Finished Arias with a shrug.

"Normally memory alteration wouldn't work on Hunters, but the blood is so diluted now it does!"

"It's actually quite handy for "resetting" failed candidates. An unexpected bonus if I do say so myself."

Lilian and Aiden looked at each other for a moment, both nervous but while Aiden was every bit as worried as Lilian was, he couldn't help being excited to have a chance to join the Hunters. It was literally a once in a lifetime opportunity which he wasn't expecting to get, but wasn't prepared to give up just yet.

"I-I don't know... " muttered Lilian as the group stopped in front of a door. "This is a lot to take in, I didn't even be-lieve in the Paranormal... well, I still don't know if I do hon-estly... and this seems kinda dangerous. Like, no offense but you guys seem really suspicious, kinda like a cult... "

Everyone nodded their head in agreement with Lilian's statement.

"She makes a good point. Good head on that one." Said Serx

"Must be her Hunter instincts." Replied Arias

"Definitely."

Acknowledging but ultimately ignoring Lilian, the pair opened the large door and they motioned for them to enter first. Which Aiden did until he found himself on the edge of a large arena like structure.

Shortly after, Lilian walked up behind him with her hand covering her face, as if she was regretting actually following Aiden into the room.

"So... "

"I think we just walked into a human trafficking circle or something." Said Lilian as she tried looking into the deep darkness that was the arena.

Only the center was lit by a single light, the source of which Aiden couldn't see and the high walls surrounding them seemed to be made of bricks but the material of the bricks was a strange black that he had never seen before.

Aiden estimated that the arena was probably one hundred meters in any direction from the center long, which made the large walls even more imposing as he thought about how they still looked humongous even from such a distance.

"Uh... maybe?" admitted Aiden as he looked back to see if perhaps the duo from earlier simply fell behind, but when no one showed up, Aiden eventually started making his way toward the center light with Lilian following closely behind, her hands gripping his left wrist.

He hadn't even heard the large door close behind him and when he thought about it, he realized that the door didn't even seem to exist as he turned in a full circle to see the whole wall was flush.

Finally reaching the center, the light shone brightly down on Aiden and Lilian when suddenly it flared out, engulfing the whole space with even, beautiful light, temporarily blinding the duo who were forced to cover their eyes.

"Welcome, prospective Hunters."

A powerful voice echoed around them and Aiden searched for its source until an area far in the distance in front of them lit up, revealing nine figures sitting on chairs.

Most of them looked like normal humans, albeit on the older side but some were like Serx and Arias, their faces a simple mask or just straight up metal faces which did little to hide the impressive aura that radiated from each of them.

"You've been selected for showing promise in the manifestation of your latent, lost abilities as a Hunter. Descendants of Dominal and Ezkiel, we are overjoyed to see promise in a bloodline we have trusted and to see the first prospective retainer of this new generation."

"Retainer?"

Aiden had never heard of the term "retainer" before in any of the books he'd read about the Hunters, be it the fiction series or any other book that referenced them. All the titles he knew of revolved around Wolf pack nomenclature.

"Seeing as you are a Retainer and Hunter combination, we will administer a modified test. We, unfortunately, won't elaborate more. Your skills, your instincts, if strong enough, will guide you to the correct answer. The dormant power that has slept for centuries, if worthy, will awaken within you as we test you now."

The one speaking, a powerful looking man with short red hair, lifted his hand up and when he did, the ground around the duo shifted until they were surrounded by multiple racks full of weapons.

"Choose your weapon. Allow your heart to guide you and let us hear your howl."

Lilian looked at Aiden and he returned her gaze, both worried as they surveyed the rows of weaponry.

From swords and axes, to crossbows, all manner of weaponry was available including flails or shields but not a single gun was among their ranks. A fact Aiden found interesting as he figured the best way to deal with the paranormal would be from a distance using a precise firearm. Not something like a bow or crossbow which could prove to be unreliable.

Feeling an affinity for one of the swords, Aiden picked it up but felt his other hand was bare and instead of a shield, ended up picking up another similar lightblade handle.

Turning them on, they burst into full, dangerous life and Aiden slowly began swinging them around, feeling like a kid again but also oddly comfortable with twisting his arms and wrists. It was strange but he felt as if the swords were an extension of his arm, but only in the most basic sense. Like a very crude prosthetic extension.

Lilian on the other hand picked up a long handle which turned into a double-sided battle axe once deployed. A heavy, powerful weapon which didn't match her petite and cute appearance, but as she swung it, Aiden saw something come over her, like some sort of animalistic bloodlust which vanished almost immediately once she noticed Aiden staring at her.

"It sort of just feels right… you know? Said Lilian, casually swinging the weapon once more, with an awkward smile.

"I guess."

"The weapons have been chosen. Let the trial commence!!"

Suddenly, the arena lights went out for a moment and when they returned, Lilian and Aiden were shocked to find a third person standing in the arena with them.

"My name is Sophia. Lone Wolf. I will be conducting your skills assessment and potential evaluation. Prepare yourself. Wolf Cubs!"

12

THE TRIAL

Sophia stared at Aiden with a soft smile before shifting over to Lilian with a similar, friendly look. Her long hair drawn back into a single braid that hung behind her almost like a tail.

At first glance, she didn't seem terribly dangerous, but for some reason or another, Aiden's body was telling him that it was in extreme danger, a fact that made his hair begin to stand on end while adrenaline began pumping through his body.

Sophia seemed to be taller than Lilian, but significantly shorter than Rosalia, her outfit consisting of a black cloak decorated with golden accents which hid everything else from sight.

"Allow me to begin." She said, as she lifted her hand into the air, the cloak lifting enough to reveal what Aiden was starting to understand was the "standard" Hunter uniform, but with some slight modifications.

But, before Aiden could take note of what those changes were, spears of fire suddenly appeared in the air.

"What in the world!?" he yelled in disbelief.

Aiden had never heard of "magic" being used to fight the paranormal in any of the books he had read. Sure, there were runes and objects that had defensive properties against the paranormal, but never was something as outlandish as bona fide magic mentioned.

"Ignitam!"

Her voice echoed as one of the spears launched forward straight at Aiden. who looked at it like a deer caught in head-lights.

But before the projectile could hit him it suddenly shattered mid-air after a flash of light intercepted it.

The sound of something hitting the ground strongly radiating from Aiden's side, he turned and saw Lilian with her axe now lodged into the ground. Her eyes sharp and focused on the Lone Wolf with a frown.

"Oh! Very nice." Clapped Sophia.

"Are you trying to kill us?" yelled Lilian as she readied her axe, adopting a stance Aiden had never seen her use before. But one she entered as if using it was second nature to her.

"No, but if one of these lands, it'll definitely sting. I'm sorry." She said, while clasping her hands together. "It's part of the test."

"This is ridiculous!"

Irritated by the confusing, irrational, and obviously dangerous situation, Lilian focused on Sophia with the sole purpose of protecting Aiden. She wasn't interested in the test or "becoming a Hunter" like she knew Aiden was. Instead, she just wanted to make sure he wouldn't get hurt trying to pass the "test".

"Ignitam!"

Another spear hurtled towards Aiden and Lilian once again swiped it out of the air.

"Stop it!!"

"It's a test. I'm afraid unless you decide to resign, it must continue."

"Then we will res… "

Stopping herself mid-sentence. Lilian thought about it and realized that if she ruined this chance for Aiden, while he might not get mad at her, he would fall into a depression over losing a chance to join a group he idolized so much, and the thought of watching him end up like that was enough for her to hold her tongue.

Even if her better judgement told her that the danger wasn't worth it.

"Ignitam!"

Suddenly, Lilian heard Aiden try and copy the "magic" the girl was using who looked at him with wide eyes before laughing.

"You've got a quick mind! Trying to use my abilities against me? Although it's not going to work. Fire elemental manipulation is my family's blood ability. I believe if you are Ezkiel's descendant… uh… try "Anim Fortus"?"

Shrugging her shoulders, Sophia pointed up and prepared to let loose another spear, her eyes shifting between Aiden and Lilian as she thought about who to throw it at next.

"Anim Fortus!!"

Not wasting a moment, Aiden took the Hunters suggestion and as the words left his mouth, he felt a very small boost of energy begin coursing through his body as a small orb appeared before him. But as quickly as the sensation had appeared, it disappeared. Leaving Aiden only more tired than before.

"Gah." Aiden gasped as he fell forward onto one knee.

"Hmmm… interesting. I thought, as a retainer you'd have more reserves to at least be able to hold your family's ability in even its weakest state. I didn't expect incompatibility. That is a very diluted bloodline."

Lilian looked at Aiden on the floor and then at Sophia who was staring at him as if he was some sort of interesting experiment or test subject.

"How does this test end, aside from us resigning?" asked Lilian.

"When the council feels like they've gotten a sufficient grasp on your potential and they declare it over, or if you somehow manage to defeat me. Although, that is unlikely, and I feel the council would end the trial before that anyways."

Looking over the floor, Lilian gripped her axe tightly and, with a deep breath, she let the energy that had started building within her since she'd picked up the axe, explode outwards.

Feeling energized, ferocious and dauntless, Lilian lunged forward with incredible strength, surprising Sophia who dodged one axe swing before landing a kick into Lilian's stomach, sending her sprawling into the dirt.

"That was close. Unexpected… rather I should have expected it considering you are of Dominal's blood line. "Dominal the Dominator" they called him. Overwhelming physical strength at an inhuman level. Less a "blood trait" though and more of a mutation that gave him monstrous power and speed."

Lilian was given a "history lesson" while she recovered from the ground and excitement started creeping up within her, which scared her due to the idea that she might somehow be enjoying violence.

The urge becoming so strong she was having trouble trying to repress it, which showed more and more as her swings became wilder and her eyes increasingly crazed.

"Definitely not at Dominal's level, but for an untrained female to wield such strength. This could probably overwhelm a lot of our rookie male hunters." Sophia continued lecturing her as she casually dodged each swing. "But you lack proper skill. Dominal's true strength came from his mastery of twin blades. His innate power was just augmentative."

Her vigor and speed increasing with each passing second, Lilian began moving at a rate that even she herself couldn't properly process. Instead, she was totally engrossed in the action of "attacking", her body moving on its own to accomplish that single task, her muscles somehow not wearing out or tiring despite the amount of energy she was exerting.

At some point though, her speed increased dramatically and the following swing caught Sophia off guard once again, causing her to, for the first time, invest her full power into blocking, having no time to dodge.

The axe blade connected with Sophia, a shockwave erupted out of the ground and dust exploded into the air, but as it settled Lilian was shocked to see a lone hand holding the axe blade between two fingers.

Sophia, with an impressed smile, was revealed as the dust settled but despite taking no damage herself, it turned out that her clothes were a different story. Her cloak was shredded from the force, leaving just her modified hunter uniform and for the first time Aiden got a good luck at her.

Unlike Rosalia's or even Serx's or Arias' uniform, Sophia's was obviously designed to be lighter.

Consisting of greaves which ended at her knees and a set of bracers for "armor", most of her outfit seemed to be skintight as it showed off her powerful, lean, and muscular physique.

There was still a certain softness to her body that made her seem less dedicated to fitness then Rosalia, but despite that there was a part of Aiden that told him she was somehow even more of an exercise-holic than her.

"I have trouble getting visible results like Hunter Rosalia." Stated Sophia as if reading Aiden's mind. "But that doesn't mean I'm physically weaker. I'm sure you'll find me significantly stronger than her." She finished as she casually pushed the axe away.

Lilian, trying to take advantage of Sophia's pause in motion to talk, suddenly felt a sharp electrical surge go through her body as she readied another swing and she fell over. Her heart rate suddenly accelerating until she couldn't hear anything side from the beat of her heart.

"Oh, I suppose that's the limit for you. That's actually really impressive. You definitely have strong Hunter genes in you."

Squatting down, Sophia picked Lilian up and looked over to the council of nine who had stayed silent the whole battle.

"We have seen enough. You can treat them both. The girl of Dominal shows enough affinity to be worth training. The boy though... we will be wiping his memory."

Shocked but not surprised after his poor performance, Aiden tried to get up but his body seemed to still refuse to properly move and instead he simply fell over, further adding to his own embarrassment which he knew was only going to grow as he felt tears begin to well in his eyes.

"I'm... not interested... in this... without... Aiden!"

Struggling on Sophia's back, Lilian willed her head to look at the council and she glared at each one individually.

"He isn't worthy. He will simply be a danger to himself and those around him. The Hunters function through trust in each other and their skills."

"Skills… are learned, aren't they?" argued Lilian. "You can't judge someone by just throwing them in a situation like this."

"We did with you, and you met our expectations. These are the requirements. Otherwise, we are simply sending unfit people to their deaths. We will not have that kind of blood on our hands!"

"Aiden is the most hardworking person I know! The most stubborn! I have no doubt that what he doesn't have in innate "talent", he will make up for with hard work! He'll be better than me! I know it! He has the willpower!" yelled Lilian.

The red-haired man standing up, he glared at Lilian with burning eyes, but as another hand grabbed his shoulder, he calmed down and returned to his seat.

"Then let us see this willpower you speak so highly of. If he can stand on his own two feet right now. We will allow him to enter training." Said a female member of the group to the left of the red-haired man. Her face obscured with a mask.

"Very well." Agreed the red-haired councilmen. "Standing after overusing his stamina to that extent would be a feat worthy of noting. Definitely not something one could do without an ironclad will and a fierce desire to battle our enemies in the dark."

"Show them, Aiden!"

Tears still in his eyes, Aiden tried to move his body, but it refused to respond.

The chance Lilian had gotten for him quickly slipping out of his hands as soon as it had shown up because he was just physically unable to perform even the most basic action of standing. But, as he laid there, with everyone watching, and with the seconds ticking by, he felt frustration grow within him. At himself.

He had the opportunity. All he would have to do was stand, but even as the frustration turned into rage, all he could do was let out a soft growl while his finger twitched.

"So. This is his so called 'willpower'." Said the man as he sat back down, unimpressed. "You'd be better off putting your faith in someone else. His inability to rise to your expectations further demonstrates his unworthiness to join our ranks."

"No! You're wrong!"

"Either you are blinded by emotion or simply lacking when it comes to intelligence. What foolishness."

"I'm... not... done!!" snarled Aiden. "Don't insult me... or... her... when you know nothing!"

His body screaming with an ungodly wail, Aiden lifted himself off the ground, his arms creaking and his muscles tearing.

A fire of rage that had shifted focus from his own inadequacies to the man who sat like a king atop a hill that had thought to insult Lilian.

Struggling to move even a centimeter, Aiden clenched his teeth to the point that his gums began to turn red while forcing his violently shaking arms to push himself up, but when he realized he wasn't making any more progress, he remembered a certain passage from the Hunter book series.

A chant that promised great strength and fortitude.

"Primordial sun. All-father of life. Conqueror of the cosmos, use this feeble body as your vessel to enact your will." Chanted Aiden.

"What's he-"

"Does he really think that'll work?"

"Fool."

"Eater of darkness, ender of all and start of life, I beseech you to grant unto me the power to overcome my trials and rise above this rabble!!"

Finishing his chant, Aiden's mind at that moment vanished for an instant but when it returned, an explosion of fire erupted from the ground around him as he became veiled in a cloak of flames.

At the same time, his hair began turning red as scales formed on the sides of his face, his ferocious, snarling but blank eyes focusing on Sophia who looked impressed while the council let out a series of gasps.

Suddenly, Aiden launched forward as fire swirled around him and where his feet left the ground but, as he got in Sophia's face, she simply smirked and unleashed a fierce head butt that immediately rendered him unconscious.

His head was thrust back violently from that single attack and he spun through the air into the ground forcefully as his momentum carried him forward.

"I think that counts." Stated Sophia, as she rubbed her slightly reddened forehead. "He invoked a spirit augmentation through incantation. A bit sloppy, but it got the job done."

"Aiden!"

Lilian tried to get off of Sophia so that she could check him, but her body was still too weak to do much more then wiggle. Leaving to her simply watch as the flames disappeared around him and turned into smoke.

"I am impressed that his call was answered at all. It is unusual for a grand class spirit like him to offer their aide to such a haphazard and pointless summoner. In fact, it's unusual for him to answer even a summons made in true distress."

"It's our refusal to worship him that makes him so unreliable in the first place. I doubt the boy knows he just summoned a grand spirit. Still, why would he answer the call of anyone outside of his "church"?"

"Perhaps the boy has some connection with Ignatious?"

"I suppose that merits allowing him to train. We can't very well turn away one who may have the favor of such a powerful elemental spirit. Especially one we've been looking to help us for centuries."

"I thought Ezkiel and Ignatious especially hated each other?"

The council members talked in hushed tones amongst themselves as Sophia walked over to Aiden's body and picked him up like a princess before moving to stand in front of the them on the arena floor.

"Enough!" ordered the red headed man. "Sophia. As a Lone Wolf, we will defer this decision to you. Seeing as how the Council cannot come to an agreement."

All eyes turned to Sophia who took a moment to examine Aiden. His previous wounds, self-inflicted or otherwise, had disappeared with the wisps of flame that had clung onto him and it seemed like aside from exhaustion, he wasn't suffering from any backlash for invoking such a great power.

"It is without a doubt that this man should be trained." She declared. "As a human blessed enough to be able to invoke a Fire elemental like myself, we cannot turn our back on he who has received the approval of one of the elemental guardians. Lest we forget that it was by their will that we gained the ability to push back against the evils born of humanities darkness."

"His skill and bloodline are lacking, but he has a connection to a grand spirit nonetheless. He is a strange one."

"Azamil, it is as Hunter Sophia says. It was the guardians that allowed us to fight, so even if he is lacking in all other aspects of being a Hunter, it is enough to have the approval of the true elementals."

"I know. But I do not like it. The elementals can be cruel at times, lending their strength to those who don't need it or shouldn't have it. This boy will see untold horrors if he joins our ranks that he is not and may not ever be ready for."

"Regardless. It has been decided."

"So, it has. The boy and the girl will begin training, be sure to prepare everything and reach out to…Hunter Rosalia, was it? The Scarletguard descendant. The one we sent to the small town to train where we found these two. She will act as their guide when their training here is complete. As inexperienced as she may be, she shows promise and if things settle down, we will send a true grey wolf in time."

The council stood up in unison and they all looked at Sophia before nodding. The Huntress bowing before going through a door that wasn't there before.

"Are all Hunter girls as fit as you?" asked Lilian.

"That's a random question… but I'd say so. Hunting the paranormal is dangerous, so it isn't like we can be picky when it comes to improving ourselves. Even if it means sacrificing our more… womanly charm. As some would say."

"I don't think it'd be a good look for me… "

"Don't worry, because of your bloodline, even if you do end up training as hard as or even harder than us, you'll always look the same... you'll keep your femininity." Said Sophia with a soft, somewhat sad smile. "You won't have to worry about men looking at you funny when you decide to wear more revealing clothes, or getting called names."

"But it's for your duty, right? Your job as a Hunter?"

"It is. But sometimes even I wish I could be more womanly."

"I think you look plenty "feminine" as is. Last I checked, there isn't anyone who can decide for you what it means to be a girl."

Letting out a small laugh, Sophia looked back at Lilian who gave her a small smile.

"I think we'll get along well." She chuckled. "You've got spunk, kid. A lot more then I did when I was your age."

"What, ten years ago?"

"Try adding a few zeroes."

"That was just a really long beauty sleep."

"That it was." Smiled Sophia.

13

NEW ROUTINE

B efore the Hunters, there existed the elementals.
Pure, flawless and uncorrupted beings represented as distinct aspects of creation.

Fire, Water, Earth, Air, Light and darkness.

These beings came into existence simply through the world continuing to exist each day, and they acted as its source for life.

The heat from the sun, the chill of ice, the breeze of the wind were the work of the great elementals acting beyond the eyes of humanity, a life form that came to be through the natural existence of the elementals.

It could even be said that humans were, in a sense, the children of these great spirits…

And, by that logic, the monsters we fight as Hunters are the children of humanity. Birthed from the darkness we all hold within our hearts and fed by our continued negative emotions.

Wrath.

Revenge.

Regret.

Jealousy.

Lust.

Once simply pollution in the pure world of the elementals, when the first of the Dark Lords came to be, it was given form. Filled with hate and unbounded evil. Birthing to life abominations.

Abominations that could not be harmed by the Elementals nor harm them, but could destroy the world the Elementals cherished while mindlessly killing their children, humanity.

Thus, the first Hunters were chosen from those willing to take up the mantle of standing against them. To act in the shadows, to put down these creatures and one day find the Dark Lords born from other similar congregations to put an end to the beings which gave human evil form.

Returning it back into it's natural, harmless state.

Reading fervently through the Hunter textbook in his hands, Aiden couldn't stop himself from continuing through it as he absorbed all the information written within its pages.

Stacked around him were piles of books from the Hunter grand library which was filled with information that had long been lost and now helped Aiden clear up multiple misunderstandings he had, along with teaching him about countless methods he had never even imagined could exist.

Lilian on the other hand, while sticking to her duty as a student, was reading at a steady, fairly bored pace. Her effort clearly going into staying focused while Aiden needed no such expenditure of energy to continue going through the countless scriptures he had been given access to as a "Hunter- in-training".

Weeks had passed since the pair's "test" at the hands of the council of nine and while at first, Lilian was still understandably still suspicious of the whole thing, she eventually was forced to accept it when their life was changed drastically for the sake of their training.

Firstly, they were temporarily "moved" to a special school which served as the main training facility for new Hunters. Originally it was a simple church, though due to a past agreement, the newly reawakened Hunters were given permission to use the land as their training grounds.

This was a fact that was very helpful in keeping new Hunters safe, considering the holy grounds of a Church were impossible for most paranormal entities to penetrate aside from the strongest among them. Namely "S-rank" entities, which the council speculated didn't exist yet.

After moving to the new school, where Lilian and Aiden had found themselves sharing an admittedly large room, they were given stacks of books and a very strict schedule to follow in regards to sleeping, eating, studying and exercise.

It was a routine that Aiden dreaded as he noticed how much physical work he would need to do daily, but one that Lilian was indifferent about, since it didn't differ much from her old routine.

In order to justify this sudden move, the Hunters called upon a few old connections that had somehow weathered the test of time and sent both of their parent's letters from their school that they were selected to participate in a "temporary student exchange program" which was an "all-expense paid trip" which would help "secure them a wealthy, comfortable future".

Aiden's mom was overjoyed at the thought of the program, simply because she had been wanting Aiden to get out more often and this would be a good chance for him to "spread his wings" as she put it, while Lilian's parents simply left the letter, signed, on the table the next day without any word, comment or notable reaction.

Which made Lilian visibly sad at first, but it all worked out in the end as Aiden's parents were both present to send them both away.

In fact, it'd be safe to say Lilian received better treatment from Aiden's parents than Aiden himself did, as they both fussed over her being prepared mentally, with the proper supplies, and she'd received a torrent of concern from the both of them.

Aiden on the other hand, simply got a thumbs up from his father and a long scolding from his mother who couldn't believe that she'd raised a son so incapable of properly preparing himself for a going away trip. A phrase she said often as she tore apart Aiden's travel case and "fixed it".

Ultimately though, with a chauffeur for the admittedly fancy transport car and a representative present, Aiden's parents still shed tears for them both as Aiden and Lilian left to go to the new school.

Once at the Church or rather "the Academy", Aiden was pleasantly surprised to see it had a lot more people than he would have initially expected for a school that trained members of an extremely secretive organization.

People from all around the world, from all types of backgrounds were there and everyone wore the same red uniform... except for Aiden, whose outfit was blue, which he later learned identified him as a "Retainer". A special type of Hunter that had the unique gift to converse with Elementals.

And while Lilian was a "normal" Hunter, the special gold trim on her uniform marked her as a Hunter with extremely high promise, a stark contrast to Aiden's bronze color trim which showed him as having poor and just barely acceptable potential as a Hunter.

Though this was something that barely bothered him, because he was simply excited about having the chance to finally realize his dream of being a real paranormal hunter.

"So, four weeks huh? Do you think it'll really work?" asked Aiden, as they sat silently in the room, reading.

"It seems strange, but I've heard of faster curriculums. Although, do you really believe all this?" asked Lilian, as she pointed to a picture of a Wendigo in the book she was reading.

"I mean... you've seen what they've done and I know you remember the Hellhounds. Plus, don't forget that fire Sophia used."

"I don't know what I remember about that day, or what I saw... " replied Lilian as she put the book down. "But if this is something you want to do. I'll support you."

"I think being a Hunter will be really cool!"

"Yeah... but don't you think you're treating all of this a bit too... lightly? This is some pretty serious stuff. If these books are true."

Aiden stopped and froze in place with a smile.

He had been so excited about the idea of the Hunters, that he hadn't considered the implications of it all, namely the very real danger they'd be facing.

It was one thing to be a passionate researcher of the paranormal, but to actually fight them? Aiden hadn't thought about it much, but it was an admittedly very big jump.

His life was now going to be on the line.

"I... think it'll be worth it. I finally have a higher purpose." said Aiden as his face became solemn. "I mean... up until now, I've just been the loser of the paranormal research club... at least this way, maybe I can be a bit cooler."

Aiden shrugged his shoulders while chuckling softly and Lilian looked at him with an understanding but sad look in her eyes.

"Oh, Aiden… "

Reaching over the table, Lilian gave Aiden a large hug, catching him off guard.

"I think you're plenty 'cool' as it is. If that means anything" she said, as she let go and sat back down. "… So, don't put yourself in danger just to be cool."

"Thanks, Lilian, but… this just seems like what I should be doing."

"Well. At least find a better reason then looking cool."

Lilian let out a sigh as Aiden returned to his book and stood up to look at herself in the large mirror that was in the middle of the room.

Looking over herself in her shorts and white tank top, Lillian put her hands on her hips while examining her figure.

After a few seconds of pinching herself to see if she'd gained any weight, she eventually put her hands under her breasts and lifted them slightly before letting out a short sigh.

"*I think they've gotten bigger again…* " she thought to herself, as she doubled tapped the center of her bra, which caused it to automatically adjust its support. "*At least I haven't gained weight anywhere else…* "

Turning around, she examined her butt and each leg. "*I wish more fat went to my butt though.*"

Poking her own behind and squeezing her leg as she searched for cellulite, blemishes, dry skin or stretch marks, Lilian nodded to herself, satisfied that there didn't to seem to be any problems.

But as she wiggled her hips, she debated about adding more lunges and squats to her workout routine.

Later, turning backward and forward and lifting an arm, she flexed her bicep and began poking the firm but still somewhat squishy muscle with her other hand.

"I wonder what Aiden will think if I become brawnier... "

Flexing her abs, despite not really having any, she poked herself and let out a small "hmmm" as she thought about what Aiden would think if she eventually got a six pack, but after a few seconds she suddenly looked up, confused with herself.

"Why am I thinking about that? Aiden doesn't care about what I look like. He'll accept me regardless. It's not like I particularly care if he likes how I look anyways..."

Shaking her head, Lilian walked over to her bed and plopped into it while crawling under the covers unceremoniously, like a cat. Where she pulled the covers over her head and curled into a ball.

"Sleeping so soon?" asked Aiden from the table. His eyes still on the book.

"Yeah, I want to make sure I get proper rest before tomorrow's first combat training session."

"You know what, you have a point, Lilian." Replied Aiden, as he closed his book and stood up. "A weary body would make for a terrible first lesson, and you know better than me that I am sorely lacking when it comes to physical fitness."

Walking over to his bed, Aiden tapped his watch a few times and his outfit turned into a pair of long, baggy pants with a baggy T-shirt to match.

He didn't usually wear pants and a shirt to sleep, but since he was sharing a room with Lilian, he didn't want to make things awkward for her. After all, regardless of how long they'd known each other, it was bound to get awkward to see him in just his underwear.

Lilian was also wearing more layers than she was used to, which she knew would end up causing her to sweat a lot as she slept, since just like Aiden, she didn't want to make things awkward for him by sleeping in her usual thin, lacy lingerie, even If he had seen her in it before.

So, with both of them slightly more uncomfortable than usual, they said their goodnights and went to sleep, the room immediately darkening as the lights turned themselves off but before Lilian was lulled off to sleep, she had one final thought.

"I bet Aiden would look good if he bulked up or gained some definition."

14

MEETING IGNATIOUS

"As a retainer, it is important to build a connection with the Elemental that has chosen you to bless with its power. Always remember to be respectful though, as you are only borrowing their strength, and you do not own it... empty your mind and focus."

Sitting cross legged on the floor, Aiden did his best to come in contact with the supposed "elemental" that he had a connection to.

According to the instructor, he had shown an "interesting" display during the exam, but Aiden had no memory of much after falling to the floor, which led him to doubt the validity of what they were saying or to take them as nothing more than just sugarcoating for his otherwise lackluster potential as a Hunter.

Still, that didn't stop him from trying and with all his might, he searched the depths of his mind for the connection to his Elemental.

"When you find the ri... "

The instructors voice trailing off suddenly as if he had been sent far away, Aiden opened his eyes to see what had happened and found himself in pitch blackness.

"Uh... hello?"

Tapping the ground to see if it was solid, Aiden was surprised to hear the sound of his foot hitting a marble floor and, as he started walking, he soon realized there was no end in sight to the pure, pitch-dark, blackness.

"Greetings, Human."

Fire erupting around Aiden, the black nothingness around him transformed into a lush, beautiful forest with a singular man sitting on top of a low hanging branch protruding from one of the trees.

He had short, ice blue hair, the left side of which was undercut and the right featured parted bangs. His was a powerful but lean build, and the aura that surrounded him made Aiden know just by looking at him, that he could be utterly oppressive.

As he jumped down, a puff of fire came out of his feet right before he landed, slowing him so that he hit the ground gently and, most impressive of all, the fire didn't burn the grass it hit, instead it actually made it grow a bit.

"A... are you my Elemental?"

Raising an eyebrow, the man let out a loud, echoing laugh that produced small embers of fire with each exhalation. The embers promptly flourishing in the air before vanishing.

"I suppose you could say that." He finally replied, walking up to Aiden who was caught off guard by his towering height.

"I… it's nice to meet you. My name is Aiden."

"Aiden… hmmm. Unconventional, you seem like more of a Fenix to me… or maybe a Dimitri? Well, anyways I'm sure you are curious as to why I have offered you my power, correct?

"A little."

"Frankly, it was your passion for what you love that caught my attention. It's not very often the burning fire of passion burns as hot as yours nowadays. It's also been a long time since someone invoked my true incantation, so when I peeked over and saw a small human full of determination calling to me, I found myself compelled to grant you my strength."

"R… really?"

"Indeed. If I made a comparison, I'd say the average human in today's day and age, as disappointing as it is since they used to be such a passionate species, is akin to this."

Flicking his wrist upwards, a small almost cute ember of fire appeared in his palm which danced in the breeze before he closed his fist, extinguishing it.

"Easy to put out. Worthless." He continued. "But yours, I'd say is more like this."

Snapping his fingers, the landscape behind him exploded into a torrent of towering flames which turned into a fearsome, whirling fiery typhoon before exploding into non- existence as the man clapped his hands together.

"I...I... appreciate the praise but, I don't think it's that big of a difference..."

"Of course, you don't, you are only human! I, on the other hand, can see more then what you can. I use more than just eyes to view the world. Although technically speaking I don't have "eyes"." He chuckled to himself.

"Y... yeah, I guess you're right... "

"Anyways. While I don't usually do introductions, that dead, lost look in your eyes tells me that you don't know that you are in the presence of Ignatious. So, just for you, out of respect for your burning HOT passion, I'll do you the honor of giving my introduction... ahem... "

Clearing his throat, Ignatious began shaking his hands and his shoulders and, after a few seconds, he threw them up into the air, causing pillars of fire to erupt behind him.

"I am Ignatious! Elemental Lord of Fire! Source of Life, beginning and the end!! Yes, that is correct, *the* Ignatious! The one worshipped by the Ignati Church!"

Dropping his arms back down to his sides, the pillars disappeared and he began rolling his wrist.

"You are free to worship me, praise be Ignatious, etcetera... etceteraaa."

"Oooh!"

Clapping his hands, Aiden made an "O" with his mouth as he stared on in awe. Something that Ignatious appreciated as he began bowing.

"Thank you, thank you. I know. I'm awesome. If I wasn't, I wouldn't have my own religion now, would I?"

"So... what do I do now?" asked Aiden, as he took a seat in the soft grass.

"Uh... I'm not sure actually. It's been a while since I really dealt with a human personally, probably a contract is needed but as long as we mutually agree... we are chill, I think that should be good enough."

Aiden blinked as Ignatious looked up at a tree branch, jumped up and sat back on it while crossing his legs.

"No... contract?"

"I think words are a form of contract. Paper wasn't always a thing, boy. So, I promise to have your back... most of the time... sometimes... occasionally? When it doesn't clash with my schedule. Yeah that'll work. I'll have your back by lending you my power when you need it when it doesn't clash with my schedule."

"Uh... ok? And in return?"

"In return, hmmm... I'm not sure. How about you sing my praises on occasion. The great Ignatious! You know, when the opportunity arises. I don't want you to be like the Church. As great as they are, they can get kind of annoying. I mean... Aye yai yai!"

JONATHAN SOLIS

Shaking his head, Ignatious threw up a small puff of fire into a tree branch and, when it disappeared, there was a ripe apple where the fire had hit which he promptly plucked and began to eat.

"Mhmph…. good apple… Mhpmph. Anyways." He started as he took bites of the instantaneously created fruit. "I suppose that should be it for our first meeting which is probably the reason the Hunters sent you to find me. We've got terms and an agreement and you've gotten to bask in my greatness."

Nodding his head slowly, Aiden had no idea if that was the whole point of the session, but his instructors had only told him that the Elemental would guide him through the process. To simply go with the flow. So, as Ignatious began waving, Aiden returned the gesture and within a few moments, the Elemental along with the landscape began to fade away.

"Wait!" yelled Aiden suddenly, causing the fading scenario to immediately regain focus.

"Sawp." Replied Ignatious while finishing the apple, core and all.

"The Hunters told me you don't like them very much. Like… you don't really help out. Why help now?"

Ignatious tilted his head and the landscape began fading again, as he let out another series of laughs.

"No reason in particular, I just felt it was time… and I found you both interesting and fun."

"So, there isn't anything really special about me to have caused you to listen to me? Aside from being passionate?" asked Aiden.

"Uh. Hm. I mean, you're a descendant for one of my biggest annoyances but…that's not really a good reason *to* answer your call. Being able to speak to my kind is pretty whatever. Anyone else could have used my chant…you know what. Don't worry so much about being "special", alright? In time, you'll learn that it's overrated."

Giving Aiden a snarky smile, he waved again and after blinking, Aiden found himself once again in the middle of the meditation hall at the school.

As his ears began registering the sounds around him, he was surprised to hear whispering around him, which he found odd until he realized that his hand was itching.

Scratching at his left hand, he looked at it and realized there was a simple mark on it, not too complex but something about it made it feel arrogant to him. As if the one who made it was so full of himself that he couldn't help but bestow a portion of that arrogance onto everything he made with his hands.

"Odd. The council told me you had spoken with an Elemental greater than a Lesser." Said the instructor as he inspected Aiden's hand. "Although it does seem different… Hmmm. What was the Elemental's name?"

"Ignatious?"

Furrowing his brow, the instructor stood up straight and put his finger under his chin to think, but after a few seconds of not reaching any conclusions, he shook his head and returned to his desk.

"That'll be all for today." Was all he said and, as Aiden got up to leave, Aiden thought he heard chuckling in the distance, but with no one else in the room, he didn't know where or who it could have come from.

* * *

"So, this is your contract with an Elemental?" asked Lilian as she flipped Aiden's hand around.

"Apparently."

"What's your Elemental's name?"

"Ignatious."

"Like… the god worshipped by the Ignati Church, Ignatious?"

"Apparently, but the instructor said that this mark represents a contract with a lesser Elemental."

"Huh, do Elementals lie?" asked Lilian as she stood up to go make some tea.

"I don't think so."

"Well, then that's great! A contract with an Elemental strong enough to be worshipped as a god? That's pretty cool."

"Thanks. Although, I'm still kinda suspicious cause of the mark and all."

"Well, don't they say that gods work in mysterious ways? Maybe your body isn't ready to handle all his power at once, so he's limiting it now, so you don't die... or something." Suggested Lilian while waving a spoon around.

"That could be!"

"Right? So how about we celebrate? How about I make your favorite?"

"Beef stew? It's been years since you've made that for me."

"Because it's been years since somethings happened to merit such a celebration!"

"We don't have a kitchen though." Mentioned Aiden as he waved his arm over the room.

"Well, actually, it would turn out there is a student kitchen in the northeast wing! We can even request ingredients and they'll be provided. What do you think?

"If you're up to it. I don't want you to do unnecessary hard work, you must be tired after all of today's training, after all."

"It isn't unnecessary. Celebrating my best friend's great news is very important to me and I'll never be too tired for the people close to me."

15

PRINCESS FIGHT

"The world we hunters live in is dangerous! Even the smallest misstep can and will most likely spell your death or worse! So, believe me when I say that if you want to survive, you better damn well listen and learn well!!"

Slamming a hand on the desk, a female Hunter with purple-streaked brown hair glared at every student inside the classroom, her stare sending shivers down the spine of anyone unfortunate enough to make eye contact with her.

"But that doesn't mean we have the luxury to act like cowards! The Hunters are the first and only line of defense humanity has against the abominations of the Dark, and while most have forgotten that due to centuries of them being vanquished, they will quickly learn how important we are if we fail! Which is a lesson I don't feel like letting them learn!"

Quickly writing down notes, Aiden underlined key phrases and Lilian simply watched the instructor attentively.

Their methods of learning were drastically different, but equally effective which was proven by the fact that the two often fought for the highest position of achievement in their normal school.

"And, does anyone here know why only we can push back the darkness?"

Immediately raising her arm, Lilian's hand cut through the air and the instructor pointed at her. Beating Aiden out.

"Lilian."

"Yes ma'am." Started Lilian as she stood up. The eyes of all the male students suddenly fixed on her. "The reason only Hunters can fight back is because of the ancient blessing of the Elementals on our descendants. It is also possible for the Elementals to bless a non-Hunter with their strength, and these individuals are called Retainers."

"Very good. Retainers are the purest form of a Hunter. All our bloodlines started with the original chosen Retainers and those who developed a close enough bond with their elementals were allowed to pass their gifts down their bloodline. It's also worth noting that when two Retainer lines combine, there is a chance for the child to manifest one of the two abilities or a new singular hybridization. Never two.

Smirking at Aiden, Lilian stuck her tongue out slightly as she took her seat and Aiden let out a hard breath as he primed his hand for the next question.

Lilian's growing grasp on her bloodline ability had given her an inhumane speed and reaction time which Aiden was finding near impossible to beat. Even if he knew the answer first, her body just outpaced his completely to the point it seemed hopeless to even try. But that didn't mean he was going to give up.

"On the topic of Bloodlines. It is important to note that they are not eternal or everlasting. If a Hunter bloodline crosses with a normal, non-elementally blessed bloodline, it dilutes it. Which starts making inheriting an ability a game of chance rather than a certainty. Which is why Hunters tend to marry within the organization and why we always keep an eye out for new Retainer lines. Despite the fact that they are extremely rare to find."

"Can the chance ever be zero?"

"No, but when the bloodline is too thin, we start getting individuals who inherit the ability but are incompatible with it. Which is a whole other topic and science that we are currently looking into since it is now, in this current era, that we have truly run into a problem like that."

The teacher still speaking, Aiden underlined the word "gamble" and sighed at the thought that he'd lost his own genetic wager.

Aiden couldn't manifest Ezekiel's bloodline ability because of his measly "2% Hunter blood". Making it so while he struck gold in inheriting it, he duded out by not being compatible with it.

Which was a real shame because from what Aiden was told, the ability had to do with using light as a projectile which was something he found extremely cool.

And it was because of his incompatibility that he was left at a disadvantage in combat training, as he had to rely simply on beginner level swordsmanship to fight, which more often than not led to him getting floored. Everyone else had at least some use of their bloodline ability.

Realistically, he could use Ignatious power so he could at least keep pace better, but he wasn't going to call on him for something so insignificant since, judging by their only encounter, Aiden felt he would get in trouble for using the "Grand Elemental" for something so pointless.

"Aiden, you've seemed eager to answer a question. So, I will ask you one that's related to being a Retainer, seeing as you are the first and only Retainer of this new generation thus far. Are you ready?"

Taking a moment to realize the instructor was talking to him, it wasn't until Lilian elbowed him that he stopped writing, looked up and noticed that he was being waited on. Her words processing at that very moment in his mind.

"Ah! Er... yes."

Chuckles broke out throughout the classroom, and Aiden felt his ears turn red, but the instructor simply stepped in front of Aiden with her arms behind her back and a stern look on her face that made Aiden gulp.

"As a Retainer… or perhaps as a Hunter who is too tired or is otherwise incapable of using their bloodline ability, how would you continue fighting a paranormal threat?"

"Depending on the threat, there are numerous runes and items one can use… from salt to things like holy water. In some cases, even running water can deter certain paranormal enemies, but in regards to the Hunter's arsenal, each Hunter can use their sigil-engraved weapon to battle most foes and it is recommended to use one's weapon as their primary form of defeating enemies."

"And why is that?" Questioned the teacher further.

"Because a bloodline ability can be very demanding of the users body. Especially over long periods of time. Along with using an Elemental's powers in the case of a Retainer. Both having the possibly to have horrific side effects if not managed correctly. But they are necessary in order to effectively battle stronger paranormal threats."

"Correct, and while most here would consider our current arsenal "obsolete", containing mainly hard light weapons, we are currently doing a lot of research on how to properly incorporate sigils into more modern weaponry like Plasma rifles. Though this, unfortunately, will take time and until we figure it out, they are useless to us since they will do nothing to most if not all paranormal entities."

Stepping back to her desk, the instructor pointed at multiple projected grids which denoted weapon grades and ability grades.

A weapon was capable of being rated from F to SSS Grade based on the number and quality of sigils on it. For abilities, a few more factors came into play, like how effective it was to the general paranormal, how effective it was against specific paranormal entities and how taxing the ability was on the user's body.

So far, Aiden had learned that Lilian's ability <Overbody Drive> was Graded as B due to its reliance on the user's skill, which didn't seem to hinder Dominal at all in the past who was a legendary Hunter with the same ability.

Ezkiel's ability <Font of Light> was considered a S-grade skill in the past, which Aiden thought would have been nice to have and, due to his elemental mark, Aiden was also informed that his "Elemental power" grade was a C.

Leaving him in a laughable state, but one that veteran Hunters told him not to worry too much about.

They'd told Aiden that "anyone capable of fighting alongside them was valuable" and that no Hunter was ever restricted by their "grade". They even went as far as to tell Aiden about the "Worst One", a legendary Hunter who was graded F, but through work and sheer willpower had reached the position of head councilmen.

It was a story that Aiden felt was a fabrication though, just to make him feel better along with any other trainees who were faced with horrible ability results.

"At least I'm part of the Hunters…"

Eventually, the midday class ended and everyone was dismissed for lunch before physical training began that afternoon. Which was something Aiden was dreading because he knew it would consist of running, weight-lifting, and today especially was reserved for swimming.

To make matters worse, a class of sparring was scheduled after physical training.

Since Hunters were expected to be able to fight in any state, be it fully healthy to near death, the academy wanted the students to get used to the sensation of battle while their bodies were on the verge of falling apart. Thus, they purposefully set up their schedules to be as grueling as possible before battle training.

This was something some took to better than others. With Aiden being one of the others and Lilian, even without using her ability, being part of the "some".

"Hey, you're Lilian, right? Me and a small group are going to be heading to karaoke for some relaxation. Want to join us?"

Sauntering up to the table where Aiden and Lilian were eating peacefully, a group of male students with friendly, but obviously fake smiles eyed Lilian rather conspicuously.

A fact that Aiden could tell was ticking her off as he noticed a very subtle twitch of her left eye, which was a giveaway, to anyone that knew her, of when she was getting irritated.

"I'm afraid I have to focus on my studies." Replied Lilian. "Normally, I would be overjoyed to partake in merrymaking but I can't very much allow myself to fall behind. After all, being unprepared could mean death!"

"Oh please, do you really believe everything they are saying here? Most of us are just here for the free food and easy credits. I've never seen a "paranormal being" in my life but these goofs came to me asking if I wanted to help contribute to something "bigger"!" laughed the one in the lead.

"Plus, it's not like you need to study as hard as you do. I believe that there is something out there and I'm ok with helping to fight it, to keep my family safe. But I think it's important to relax every now and again as well. Too much stress wears out the body, you know?"

Another boy who looked much more reasonable than the leader offered his opinion and Lilian looked at him with a slightly softer expression, noticing that unlike the others he was making eye contact with her and most likely genuinely looking to unwind rather then pick up girls.

"I understand. But I'm afraid I'll still have to say no."

Letting out a sharp click of his tongue, the leader looked at Aiden as if he had just noticed that he existed, a look coming over his face as if he had just thought of a great idea.

"Ah, you're... Aiden, right? You should join us. It'll be fun!"

"You just want me to go with you so I convince Lilian to come along." Stated Aiden as he took a bite from his small loaf of bread. A ping of annoyance growing inside Aiden as the other guy continued to harass Lilian. "You don't really care if I go or not, but unfortunately for you, I don't control Lilian. She is her own person."

A scowl coming over his face, the man suddenly launched his arm forward and grabbed Aiden by the collar but before he could do anything else, Lilian had already shot up and put her fist at his throat.

"I think we are all reasonable people here." She said calmly. "But, if you think threatening my friends will make me want to spend any sort of time with you, I suggest you see a therapist."

Letting out a sigh, the man let go of Aiden's collar and walked away with a sharp turn of his head, his group going with him, but as they left the reasonable one from earlier looked back and gave Lilian a quick apologetic gesture.

"Sorry." sighed Aiden as he fixed his collar and examined his clothes which had been stained from his plate being flipped in the scuffle.

"For what?" replied Lilian, as she took out a napkin and began helping Aiden clean himself.

"The fact you have to stick up for me. I should be able to fight my own battles."

"Aiden, I'd rather hear you say thanks and even then, I'd still be insulted. Even if you can fight them, it's not like I'm going to let you go at it alone. Besides, they got mad at you because of me. I should have been sterner when I turned them down. Beat around the bush less."

"No, I like you the way you are now. Nice to everyone until they try and pick a fight. If you start responding nasty right from the get go, it just wouldn't seem like you."

"I suppose." Chuckled Lilian, as she fixed Aiden's blazer.

Unlike normal clothes which were projected using nanobots, Hunter uniforms had to have a singular, solid state, like traditional clothes, in order to properly imbue them with defensive runes and effects. Thus, Aiden and Lilian were learning of the things people of the past had to deal with like "cleaning and washing."

Their first experience with a washing machine leaving both of them exhausted and confused.

* * *

Later on, during training, Aiden learned that school with the Hunters was, in fact, still very much like normal school as the trainee from earlier chose him to spar.

"I want to fight that guy. The one Lilian is always hanging around for some reason." He said, as he pointed his lance at Aiden, who until that point was doing sets of swings with his swords to further develop his muscle memory.

"What?"

"I'm going to show Lilian why I'm better than you, and exactly how. Once I wipe the floor with you it'll show her just who she should be spending the most time with" declared the man, whose name Aiden found out was Marx.

"When has this ever worked... not even in books... " muttered Aiden as he walked over to the combat circle that had been the home of many, humiliating defeats for him in the last few days.

"Let's go." Challenged Marx, as he waved his lance in a figure eight in Aiden's direction.

Deploying his swords, Aiden hunkered down into his fighting stance and spent a few extra seconds making sure his posture was right before nodding. The instructor then rose his arm to signal the start of the sparring match which was followed by a horn.

"Take this!!"

Instantly charging at Aiden, Marx pulled his lance back and stopped inches away from Aiden who had brought his swords up to defend himself, but in response Marx quickly squatted down, whipped around and kicked upwards, sending Aiden into the air.

Meanwhile, Lilian watched from a distance with sweat dripping over her face, having just won her own sparring match. Worried for Aiden who was now airborne.

Aiden on the other hand, was surprised by the lack of pain he felt from the attack as he landed a few feet away, a bit shaken but otherwise unharmed and, as he looked at his forearm, he noticed that his sigil was glowing dimly.

"*Is that your way of saying you'll help me?*" asked Aiden, hoping his thought would reach Ignatious.

"*He is annoying.*"

Not saying anything else, Aiden felt an instinctual urge to lift his arm and as he did, he saw a small spurt of fire blow out of his hand.

"Woah." He said, as he watched himself produce flames for the first time, but Marx didn't give him much time to admire his own achievement as he ran forward and began bombarding Aiden with a series of blows from the side of his lance, knocking him from side to side until he was once again in the air and then kicked away once more.

"I heard you contracted with a lesser elemental, but for that to be the extent of its power, that really must be a lesser elemental. A weakling among weaklings!" laughed Marx as he spun his lance in preparation for his next assault.

"*That's it. I'm taking over.*"

"*You're what?*"

Ignatious voice ringing in his ears, Aiden's body suddenly moved on its own and he landed cleanly on the ground after doing a graceful flip.

"Arrogance boy. Your insolence will cost you." Growled Ignatious using Aiden's voice. Getting an amused look from Marx.

"Nova Armor!!"

Spreading his arms out, Aiden exploded into flames that wrapped around his body. Cloaking him completely in fire and melting the surrounding area.

"W.. what is that?!" Gasped Marx in horror, as he nervously took a step back.

A deadly look came over Aidens' face as his iris's became more serpentine in nature. Frightening Lilian who had never seen him make a face like that before.

"I'll show you a 'Lesser spirit'." Growled Aiden.

"Torrent sky!!"

A blast of wind shot out of Marx and struck Aiden whose mouth twisted into a smile as the attack only served to increase the strength of the fire wrapped around him.

Now in front of Marx, the flames from Aiden began licking at his opponent. Burning through his armor layer by layer like a hot knife through butter despite the fact the fire was only lightly grazing him.

"*Ignatious, you need to stop.*" Warned Aiden as he began to worry about Marx's safety, a cue that Ignatious picked up on and found irritating.

"*Stop? He would dare insult the Lord of Flame and think he can get away with a simple scare? He must learn respect.*"

"He doesn't know!"

"*He needs to learn respect for the Elementals. No human has any right to look down upon any of us.*"

Aiden's thrust his arm backwards, his hands clenched as if he was gripping onto a ball.

"Draco Meteor!"

Immediately, fire appeared in his hand but as Marx watched it turn into a small ball, he let out a snicker, thinking that he was getting scared over nothing, but just as his confidence was reaching a level where he thought he could talk, the small orb in Aiden's hand exploded into a ball of raw flames the size of a quarter of the combat circle, the fires touching the edges of the barrier meant to keep spectators safe and promptly destroying it where the two met.

"You will learn respect for the Elementals and suffering will be your teacher!" Hissed Ignatious, as Aiden, putting his forehead up to Marx's who was only looking at the wall of fire in front of him.

"Stop!!" yelled the teacher as he ran forward, noticing that things had gotten far out of hand.

"Stop?! Who are you to order me to cease my lesson in respect?" Asked Aiden as the ball of fire disappeared, leaving behind black floors and steam.

"You must be Aiden's elemental." Said the teacher cautiously. "I apologize for this student's transgression, for his insulting of you, oh great fire Elemental. Please, retire for today and allow us humans to punish him accordingly."

"You expect me to believe that dribble? Your organization has never been strict enough with your trainees and that's why these things happen. You do not teach them proper respect for us!!"

"*Ignatious! Enough*!" Yelled Aiden, as he began to try and wrestle control of his body from Ignatious.

"*Silence! You dare try and stop me?*"

"*You are going too far!! This isn't ok! Is that really the kind of image you want to set for the "Great Ignatious"? Huh!? Irritable, dangerous, uncontrollable? Not cool!?*"

"*Not... cool?*"

Aiden's arm dropping to his side as the instructor continued to try negotiating with Ignatious, who wasn't even paying attention anymore, and the Elemental looked at his hands before squinting his eyes.

"*Nonsense! There is no greater "cool" then being able to bend the weak to your will with overwhelming strength!*"

"*Just chill!*" Pleaded Aiden.

Letting out an irritated growl inside Aiden's mind, Ignatious sighed and Aiden felt his body start to relax.

"Very well. Since we have only just made our agreement, I'll let this be a chance for you to act as my envoy and punish blasphemers in my steed. This time, I will allow him his life, but next time he or anyone else dares to insult me, I expect you to de liver proper punishment, else I will do it myself."

"I… I'm not your envoy. I'm your partner…"

"Right…"

Suddenly disappearing from his body, Aiden almost fell over as he regained control of himself and, when the instructor noticed, he let out a long sigh before wiping the sweat from his face.

"It would seem you got a short-tempered Elemental, Aiden." Laughed the instructor nervously, as he quickly checked on Marx who had passed out. "This happens from time to time. Elementals can be prideful, especially fire-based ones. But no worries, in time, those 'involuntary' take overs won't happen as often."

Aiden nodded his head and looked over to Lilian, who was now standing at the very edge of the circle, ready to run in.

"So, it'll get better?"

"Of course! I'm sure it was scary for you, but as you two work together, you'll get a better understanding and reach a common ground. Elementals aren't bad after all."

Taking the instructors words to heart, Aiden rubbed the side of his arm as he left the circle and almost immediately Lilian jumped on him and began spinning him, looking for wounds or other kinds of damage to his person.

"You ok?" she asked while grabbing his shoulders.

"A bit shaken, but I think I'll live." Replied Aiden with a weak laugh.

Suddenly, Lilian put her face to Aiden's and looked him straight in the eye, her lips almost touching his.

"I don't know who you think you are, Elemental. But if you keep forcing Aiden to do things he doesn't want to do, I'll find a way to find you and teach you a thing or two! You hear me?"

"*Tell her I hear her.*"

"He says he hears you." Repeated Aiden.

"Good! So, you better watch yourself, mister!"

"*I like her. She's got some spice. Very attractive by human standards, too.*"

"*Don't get any funny ideas.*" replied Aiden flatly and coldly to Ignatious, who felt a wicked smile play on his lips as he felt the chill behind Aiden's usually submissive voice. "*Besides, she just threatened you, aren't you suppose to get angry.*"

"*She is sticking up for a friend. Not out of arrogance like that other brat. That is commendable.*"

"I don't get you."

"You don't need to."

Letting out a sigh, Aiden left the ring and looked back at the instructor who now had Marx thrown over his shoulder.

"Take a break in your dorm, Aiden. Elemental possession of that scale is very taxing on a body especially if it isn't used to handling such power. I'm honestly quite impressed you're still standing."

"Really? I don- "

THUD.

16

PRINCESS REVENGE

"Sparring match, Lilian versus Marx… begin!!"

The instructor lifted his hand into the air to mark the beginning the match and Marx let out an audible gulp as he took a single step back to dodge Lilian's large battle axe. Which had taken no time to near him.

Following Ignatious possessing Aiden, it would turn out that not only was his body not ready to unleash that level of Ignatious's Elemental strength which he called "but a mere drop of the ocean he wielded", but also, his body was not conditioned enough to handle the strength with which Ignatious moved his limbs.

Thus, Aiden ended up in the medical ward for a few days with severely torn muscles across most of his body which were only bearable due to him being comatose from the immense stamina over-expenditure. Ignatious had accidentally overlooked that factor when using him as his vessel and was currently making up for by supplying a bit of his energy to keep Aiden from dying of literal exhaustion.

And while this could all mostly be attributed to Ignatious's carelessness with Aiden, from Lilian's point of view, it was all Marx's fault and because of the critical state that Aiden was now in, her rage was uncontainable.

So, as soon as it was time to spar the next day with Aiden still unconscious, she didn't spare a second to challenge Marx, who came out of the ordeal with a serious scare, but otherwise unscathed.

And while Marx did his best to protest, in the end, he was forced to take the match.

"You're mine now." growled Lilian as she brought her axe up.

Normally, Marx would say something witty or sarcastic, but he found himself unable to speak and it wasn't because Lilian was on his "hit list" of girls to sleep with, it was because there was something about her current state that unnerved him and made him genuinely fear for his life.

It was nothing compared to the aura he had felt from Aiden but it still shocked him to get overwhelmed with such bloodlust from the refined, cute and ever elegant Lilian.

The "Golden Princess" as she was often called amongst most everyone else.

Luckily for him though, in his favor were his reflexes, which allowed her to block or dodge her axe swings but, he soon realized how bad blocking was as his arms were thrown

to the ground as Lilian's axe violently forced his lance down into the floor.

Now stuck there, Marx tried to pull it out to no avail, only to get his vision filled with Lilian's foot as she jumped into the air and delivered a fierce roundhouse to his face, knocking him straight into the edges of the barrier wall with a loud "Thwom!".

Landing gracefully on the ground, Lilian quickly flicked her hair before spinning her gargantuan weapon as if it weighed nothing more than a stick, her eyes narrowing like those of a predator stalking down its prey as they seemingly glowed under the arena light.

"If you insist on fighting me, I'm not going to go easy on you!" yelled Marx, as he shook his head while leaning against the wall.

Hoping to buy some recovery time with words, he let out a sharp "eek!" as Lilian's axe imbedded itself into the ground and barrier as she forcefully threw it at him, just barely missing his face.

Lilian had no more words and had no desire to find any.

For the first time in a long while, she was seething and the object, the target of her rage was simply waiting idiotically, seemingly willing to accept her judgement.

"I warned you!" yelled Marx.

His face straining, gusts of wind whipped around Marx as he began using his bloodline ability.

"Feel the wrath of my Tempest storm! A bloodline ability that allows me to manipulate air currents!"

The current picking up as Marx swung his arms, Lilian scoffed and seemed extremely unimpressed by his display as she began charging through the air without any visible hinderance before thrusting a powerful knee into her enemy's stomach.

"Gah!"

Going a few inches into the air, Lilian grabbed his collar and flipped him over her shoulder, throwing him almost to the center of the sparring zone, where he continued sprawling through the ground until he managed to catch himself.

"Impossible!"

<Tempest Storm> was an A grade bloodline ability which was used in the past by a Hunter named Kat. Allowing the user to manipulate wind currents, Kat was capable of creating blades, walls, and even whole storms using her ability which was considered one of the purest bloodline abilities of them all when it came to mimicking an Elemental's power.

Unfortunately for Marx though, even with his innate talent for using the ability, his <Tempest Storm> was currently only at a level of hindering physically weak individuals and buffeting others. More specifically, it was currently at a level where it just created a simulation of a windy plain.

Even concentrating the wind for his "attacks" only did as much as a push or shove, which, when combined with his lance skills could be good at creating openings but into Lilian, whose <Overbody Drive> increased her strength and speed, it was astonishingly useless.

"Tempest!!"

A gust of wind hitting Lilian, she stopped in front of Marx as she blew a breath of air at her bangs.

"Congratulations, you fluffed my hair."

Putting her fists up, Lilian threw a punch at Marx but was caught off guard when he threw his arm up and his lance scratched the side of her training outfit.

"Now, you'll see why you should have stuck with me!" jeered Marx.

Letting loose a flurry of jabs, Lilian was forced to step back as the number of attacks overwhelmed her and her still developing sense of battle, causing her to almost trip and despite her increased speed and strength, she could feel her body beginning to tire out, meaning she had to finish the match soon or face humiliation.

Humiliation in failing to get revenge for Aiden again. Like she always did. Because what she cared about wasn't winning or losing, it was making Marx pay for his part in having Aiden ending up how he did.

Using what little she had learned about fighting in the short time she had been at the academy, Lilian continued jumping back to dodge Marx's consecutive strikes but it wasn't until she hit the barrier that she realized that she had positioned herself exactly where she wanted to be.

Ducking, Lilian jumped and grabbed her axe from the barrier, ripping it out and, as she dug her feet into the ground to stop her momentum, she quickly turned and threw the axe straight at Marx whose eyes went wide as the large weapon spun toward him.

Putting up his lance to block, the loud screech of breaking metal exploded out of Marx's weapon as Lilian's axe destroyed it and the subsequent force went through his chest, stopping his heart for a moment.

His vitals registering as "red" for an instant, the automatic system of the sparring circle immediately blared its horn and deactivated all the weapons within it. Bringing the match to a stop just as the head of Lilian's now deactivated weapon smacked Marx across the face.

"That's it! Match is over!" declared the instructor, as he walked up with his arms outstretched and stood between two Hunters.

Looking at Marx, who had fallen over while holding his face, but still conscious, and Lilian who was panting heavily, the teacher nodded his head once before putting his arms down.

"Good spar." Praised the instructor. "Although, Lilian, I understand you are upset from yesterday's events, but it is important for a Hunter not to let themselves be guided by sheer emotion. Especially anger. We don't personally care how much you beat each other up in sparring because what you'll experience in the field will be one hundred times worse, but make sure you keep a level head. Understood?"

"Yessir." Said Lilian with a short bow in between deep, ragged breaths.

"And you, Marx. Try not to make your comrades hate you. We are all here fighting for the same cause. One day you will need their help. Without a doubt. Best make it easier for them to agree to help you than not, aye?"

Giving Marx one last glare, Lilian stepped off the platform to the sound of multiple girls cheering and congratulating her on her win. Many of them jumping up and down as they admired her powerful display of battle prowess.

For some reason, she always attracted circles of "admirers" and while she had gotten used to it, she never understood why it happened. Although that wasn't to say that she didn't like it. Unless they were people who didn't understand boundaries or the word "no".

"That was amazing out there, Lady Lilian!"

"As impressive as always Lady Lilian!"

"Thank you, everyone. But I'm just like all of you. I'm learning, I'm sure there are many among you here who could do better than I."

"Impossible!"

"Unbelievable!"

The crowd continued cheering for her as she left to go wash up, but before exiting the room, Lilian let out a small sigh and gave them all her signature smile. Earning an explosive resurgence of cheers.

* * *

"So, how long am I going to be stuck here?"

"Who knows. However long it takes for your body to recover I suppose. Luckily, I saved your mind through our connection so, you can at least do something here in the mentalscape while waiting."

Sitting on a grassy plain, Aiden tried making a crown of flowers using a large beautiful pasture that Ignatious had created to complete the same task, the Lord of Fire humming happily as he carefully produced crown after crown.

"So, when I was reading about the Hunters, there was a lot of stuff about sigils and tools. Normal things people could use to defeat the supernatural. But, so far, the academy has only taught us about using their weapons, Elementals and "bloodline" abilities. Not really much emphasis on things like salt, holy water or anything else. Why is that?"

Looking up from his crown, Ignatious' smile turned into a slight frown and he sighed deeply while looking out over the horizon.

"That's just how the Hunters do things. I tried to tell them in the past that creations of humanity can be defeated by the creations of the earth. Specifically, that paranormal creatures have natural enemies within nature. but they are an arrogant organization. They refuse to believe they are not as special as they believe. They don't understand that we made them as a temporary solution while the earth made its own."

"What do you mean?"

"It's in those books you read. For example, the werewolf is weak to silver and phantasms are weak to salt. Vampires to sunlight. That sort of thing."

"Ah."

"The Hunters do not wish to adapt or share their knowledge and be forgotten. They refuse to give up their mantle of being 'special' and the 'defenders of humanity'."

"That doesn't sound like the Hunters I read about."

"Don't believe everything you read, boy. The other Elementals are just as arrogant, refusing to acknowledge the Hunters went against their initial plans. That sort of arrogance to me is simply foolishness… so, in order to fix our mistake, I did what has caused me to be ostracized by my brethren… I created a church."

"I thought that was just to have people praise you and stuff?" asked Aiden, as he looked down at his poorly made crown and set it aside with its other deformed brethren before trying again on a new one.

"I enjoy being worshipped as much as any sentient being, don't get me wrong! But that isn't the main reason. I created the church as an organization that could fight evil without the use of bloodlines or Elementals. My brethren don't agree with that last part very much." Laughed Ignatious as he examined his crown. "... But what do I care."

"Then how do they fight? I thought only bloodline abilities were truly effective against paranormal beings. With Sigil weapons being decent, but less then optimal. Stuff like salt just being more like hinderances to buy time."

"That's a lie fed to you by the Hunters. My church proves that as they fight using those very things to defeat monstrosities. They also use sigils which call upon the natural energy of the world. Another unpopular method of mine since anyone can use them if drawn correctly."

"I tried doing that once, but it didn't work."

"That's because it was a Hunter sigil. They will not work because those are created to rely on Elemental energy to function. If the maker has no elemental energy, then it's just a pretty picture."

Aiden looked at Ignatious as he continued nonchalantly making his crowns, conflicted on whether to believe him, or the organization he had only ever dreamed of joining.

", I can sense your conflicting feelings, so allow me to clarify that they aren't bad. They do help humanity. Which is why the church has always supported them and worked together with them. We just…have different ideals. For example, I dislike them for their exclusivity of knowledge."

"And if they weren't so secretive about…well, their secrets?"

"They'd have an army like my church with warriors capable of doing the job of five Hunters per one person."

"Are you sure you aren't just tooting your own horn?" replied Aiden with a small smile, as he finally made a somewhat decent crown.

"I taught them how to use the unlimited resources available to them. So, I'd say no, I'm being quite factual. Unlike the Hunters who use a "one solution fits all" approach, my church knows the most effective way to defeat every single paranormal being to exist thus far. We don't just rely on brute force."

"So, you don't help the Hunters personally because you have different ideologies then? But you are willing to support them, because you fight a common evil? That seems reasonable to me."

"You'd be surprised how few actually understand that. Although, I had a feeling you might. Looking into your life a bit, I see you have a true passion for the paranormal and an admirable sense of righteousness and justice. Weak in body you may be, even in mind… but in spirit you have me impressed."

"Thanks?" replied Aiden as he tried to make the best of the perhaps unintentionally backhanded compliment.

"Anyways. I sent a "divine message" to my church to send a healer for you a bit ago."

"A healer? Wait, how long have I been in here?"

"Too long, hence why I sent for a healer. She's quite good at what she does. Although, I'd recommend being a bit wary around her, especially if she finds out that you have a connection with me. Ok?"

"Uh... "

"Anyways."

Flicking his wrist, Ignatious sent Aiden away and he once again found himself waking up suddenly, in the academy medical ward, with a pair of yellow eyes staring at him from less than an inch away.

"Hi, my name is Catarina Ekatarina. Sister of the church of Ignatious, a pleasure to meet you, chosen of the Lord of Flame."

Gulping, Aiden simply returned her gaze and, as she slowly backed away, her smile, while kind, sent a chill down his spine. Her unwavering eyes slightly unnerving Aiden until she suddenly stood up and left without saying another word.

"I just realized I might have called you my 'contracted human'." Confessed Ignatious, with a laugh. *"Well, good luck."*

17

FOLLOWER OF IGNATI

"Gwahaaa!!!!!"

Letting out a loud yell, causing the room's walls to immediately enter "sound canceling" mode so his scream wouldn't disturb the other people sleeping the dorm, Aiden stared, confused and scared by a pair of yellow eyes that he had discovered under his covers.

"What's going on!?!"

Hearing Aiden scream, Lilian immediately jumped out of bed in her sleep wear, her axe already deployed, ready to swing as she searched the room for what had caused Aiden to yell so loudly, but as her eyes became transfixed on an unusual lump around his abdomen, she slowly lowered her weapon and narrowed her eyes.

"Good morrow, chosen of Ignatious. I hope you did sleep well." Said Catarina casually, as she straightened her back out while still sitting on Aiden, who quickly realized that she was still wearing her nun's garbs.

Scrambling out of the bed, Aiden slammed the side of his head into the floorboards and Lilian stood next to him while glaring at Catarina.

"Aiden, who is this?"

"I-I-I don't kno-"

"Hello, I apologize for my late introduction. My name is Catarina Ekaterina. Devout follower of the Ignati."

Stepping off Aiden's bed, Catarina stood up and did a small bow.

"Ignati? Why is a nun of the church coming into a man's room?" asked Lilian, as she stepped in front of Aiden.

"Because that man is the chosen envoy of Ignatious and as a follower, I have been chosen to act as his confident. His right-hand woman so to speak... in every sense of the phrase."

Giving Lilian a small smile as she tilted her head, Catarina tapped the middle of her chest and her nun outfit ironed itself out along with the habit.

"Huh? Aiden doesn't need a right-hand woman! If Aiden needs something, he has me. He doesn't even know you, he can't trust a weird woman who just crawls into his bed unannounced!"

Squinting her eyes, Catarina's smile wavered for a moment as she put her hands over her lap, Aiden noting that she squeezed her hands together after she did.

"I'm afraid I can't allow that. I am a pure, clean woman of the church. Promised to Ignatious and his chosen representative on this world. I cannot accept a woman like you as his confident. After all, with a body like that I can only imagine how many men you have bedded. How can such a dirty woman like you stand by the pure chosen of Ignatious?"

"B… bedded? I'll have you know that I haven't 'Bedded' anyone!" replied Lilian, her calm tone breaking into indignation.

"Mhm, is that so? Regardless, you are not qualified."

"More than you! You don't even know anything about Aiden!"

"I know enough. I know he is Ignatious' chosen, and that is all I need to know. I am well versed in how to properly care for a man and meet their needs. Although admittedly I lack… hands on experience, but I am sure the gracious chosen of Lord Ignatious will have patience with me."

"Aiden isn't looking for a fling! Or a girl to casually sleep around with!"

Getting closer to Catarina, Lilian was now frowning and as the tension continued to build, it wasn't until Aiden stood up and got between them that things started to deescalate.

"W-wait! Hold up!" he declared loudly, as he used his hands to gently push the two away from each other. "Catarina, I appreciate your commitment to your church, but I'm not really in need of a 'right-hand woman' right now. Ok? You can tell your church bosses and I'll have a word with Ignatious about it."

"But… "

"No buts. It's making things awkward. and Lilian isn't happy about this and if Lillian is upset, I get upset."

"Is she your lover? Is that why you live together?"

"No, we are just really close friends, and like a good friend, I'm not going to allow a situation that's making her angry to continue if there is anything I can do about it. OK? So, please? You seem like a nice girl, so I don't want to sound too mean but if you really need to, we can talk about this later."

A look of pain came over Catarina's eyes, she lowered her head and her habit's shadow hid her eyes from Aiden, who didn't think his words would have such a drastic effect on her.

"As you wish."

Bowing, Catarina made her way to the door, but as she left, Lilian felt a sharp chill go up her spine as Catarina shot her a glare that made her skin crawl.

"That's a… character." Said Lilian as she shook off the goosebumps.

"Sorry about that. It wouldn't be a church without zealots, right?"

"I guess, but you should be careful, she seems dangerous, and she somehow managed to come in here despite the door being locked."

Aiden looked at the door to his room and realized that Lilian had a point, the security of the rooms was top notch, so a stranger certainly shouldn't have been able to break in like that. Yet, as Aiden examined both the door and locking mechanism, he couldn't find any sign or trace of forced entry. It was as if Catarina had just appeared inside.

"I'll check the registry."

While going through the list of people who have access to the room Aiden couldn't find any sort of mystery person or extra name on the list. The roster consisting of only himself, Lilian, and the school staff in charge of dorm management.

"That's kind of creepy." whispered Lilian, who was looking through the list over Aiden's shoulder.

Nodding his head in agreement, Aiden looked out the window to see what time it was and, with the sun starting to rise over the horizon, he decided he might as well start his day, even if it was a bit earlier then he was used to.

"Breakfast?" asked Aiden, wanting to forget about the whole incident and move on.

"I'd love to." Replied Lilian with a smile, as she toggled through a few outfit options in the mirror, finally settling on a light blue summer dress she enjoyed wearing. "Let's go."

* * *

"Sparring match! Aiden vs Lilian! Start!!"

"Uh… "

"Er… "

Staring at each other with awkward looks, both Aiden and Lilian remained locked in place as the Instructor threw their hand up into the air to mark the start of the match.

Today was the day students had to face off against students they hadn't sparred with before and, naturally, that meant that despite their best efforts not to, Lilian and Aiden had to battle it out.

Neither of them could bring themselves to make a move as everyone watched them eagerly until Aiden finally drew his blades and locked eyes with Lilian, causing her to step back.

"Let's go!" yelled Aiden as his knuckles turned white from gripping his swords so tightly.

Aiden had spent so much time trying to protect Lilian that it seemed almost counterproductive to want to fight her, but in this situation, he wasn't going to back down. He had to show her that he was capable of helping her in her time of need. He wanted to show her that he wasn't a weakling. A thing for her to protect. He wanted her to see him as a real warrior, one capable of protecting those important to him.

Lilian on the other hand, had no intention of fighting Aiden, the thought of lifting her axe against him alone, caused her to lose the will to fight and, while she didn't show it on her face, the relaxed grip on her weapon gave away her intentions to resign to Aiden.

"I-I don't want to fight you Aiden." She murmured.

"Neither do I, but this is practice."

"You'll get hurt… "

Aiden bit his lip as Lilian gave him a sad look, but he shut off his conscious as he refused to let his reasoning dictate his movements. Eventually leading to him charging forward.

"Raaaa!!"

Closing the gap between them, Aiden swung his blades while yelling but as the last moment, he diverted them and struck the ground right next to Lilian.

"I… can't."

Standing up straight in front of Lilian, she offered him a small smile, but before Aiden could say anything a hand cut between them and the instructor pushed them away from each other.

"This is sparring. There are no friends. You will never survive as a Hunter if you let yourself be controlled by emotions like this. There have been times Hunters have had to kill their friends who have turned into creatures of unimaginable horror… and there are Hunters who have died because they could not do so."

Looking at both of them, the instructor took a step back and threw his hands up into the air once more.

"Match resume!"

But, once again they failed to strike at each other until Aiden noticed Lilian pick up her axe.

"This is just sparring." She said to herself. "Just... sparring."

She threw a half-hearted swing at Aiden, who dodged it with relative ease and Lilian looked over at the crowd which was starting to go silent and become agitated.

"Lilian, if we do this. We do it right. No holding back!" Declared Aiden as he crossed his swords.

"Y-you might get... "

"I'm not a thing you own that needs to be protected all the time! If you respect me as your friend and as a man, come at me right NOW!!"

Doing his best to put on a mean face, Aiden glared at Lilian who straightened her back and then looked back at Aiden with eyes that sent a chill through his body. Her red eyes having taken on a glow that Aiden only ever saw when she was serious about something.

He could feel the creeping chill of fear begin to wrap around him as his mind brought forth memories of all the sparring matches that Lilian had been in, how ruthless she could be and how overwhelming her power was. But as terror tried to grip his heart, he steeled his resolve.

"I'm not going to fall behind. Let's go Lili-"

Lilian suddenly appearing inches from him, she swung her axe with an emotionless face and Aiden just barely managed to dodge her strike as her axe broke through both of his weapons.

Stepping back, Aiden gritted his teeth and threw his knee at Lilian's exposed stomach but before his knee was anywhere near her, she was already next to him and with a swat had sent him spiraling toward the barrier wall where he crashed into it with a hard "Thwoom", generating a wave of cheers from the spectators.

"Amazing! That's our Princess!"

"Lady Lilian! Fantastic work!"

Aiden slid to the floor, his body shaking from that single strike despite not having taken any real damage. Making it painfully obvious just how large the power gap between him and Lilian was.

Punching the ground, Aiden stood back up and redeployed his swords, repairing the damage to the blades as they reformed, but before he could look for Lilian, she was already in front of him, driving her knee into his chest.

"oof!"

Thrown into the air as a blast of air exploded from the contact point from the force she'd let out. Aiden wasn't even given a chance to react as Lilian grabbed his ankle and threw him back down again, this time toward the middle of the arena where he hit the ground and skidded on his back before finally coming to a stop, splayed out in all directions like a rag doll.

"*Heh. She isn't holding back. Although, I feel you getting frustrated right now, hm, Boy?*"

"*Not at her, at myself. I want to prove to her that I can protect her and myself, I don't want to be seen as the protected anymore!*"

"*Sometimes it is better to realize you are weak and let those who are strong, those who are your allies do the work.*"

"*I'm not weak!!*"

"*Face your reality...*" growled Ignatious. "*Or... you can try your hand at reforging it. If you think you have the determination and fire to do so.*"

Standing up, Aiden brought his arms up just as Lilian came up again, only to bat his arms away with two kicks before quickly spinning and landing a third into his chest, sending him flying back through the air again.

"*Reforge... myself?*" thought Aiden as he flew through the air.

"*If you can.*"

Bursting into flames, Aiden landed on the ground with a hard thud, surprising Lilian and the Instructor, who was getting ready to intervene as he thought Aiden had lost control of his Elemental again.

But as Aiden rose his hand, the teacher realized that the fires wrapped around him were much weaker than the last time. Appearing to have been tamed and controlled.

"*A good start. But that puny fire will not even heat the soul on a cold day, let alone allow it to be remade.*"

" *Everyone starts somewhere.*"

"*That they do.*" Replied Ignatious, a sensation washing over Aiden that made him feel like Ignatious was smiling.

Running forward, now cloaked in a light fire, Aiden unleashed a powerful punch that Lilian casually sidestepped, but ended up being caught off guard as Aiden's other arm drove a fist into her side, sending her sliding back a few feet with a trail of fire in her wake.

Surprised, Lilian looked at her uniform which was slightly charred and then at Aiden who got back into a fighting stance.

And together, they shared a wide toothy smile.

Electricity and fire exploded into the air as Aiden's sword met Lilian's axe, her blade cracking slightly from the force, something she had never seen before and a event that made her blood boil even more as she watched Aiden's continue to press the attack.

A strange urge came over her then. An almost animalistic sensation that began driving her movements, willing her to fight harder, move faster and be fiercer.

Lilian's eyes for the first time locked onto Aiden like she'd done with Marx, her bloodlust exploding outwards but unlike the other times where her opponents would be overwhelmed, this time, Lilian found herself matched by a hot, burning passion that radiated out from Aiden.

A fact that made her even more excited in a way she couldn't explain.

For years, she had stood at the top of everything she did.

For years, people would bow to her and treat her like a queen.

And as for how many years it had been since she had faced a truly fierce competitor... she couldn't remember. All she knew was that she had ached for a rival for the longest time and, as she lifted her axe again, she looked at Aiden and remembered how they'd met so many years ago.

18

MEMORY OF INNOCENCE

"Mommy! I'm scared!!"

"It's ok, Lilian! It's just a slide. Just slide down and push and you'll go straight down! You'll be ok!"

"I'm scared!!"

Standing at the top of a slide with shaky legs, a six-year-old Lilian had tried desperately to gather the courage to go down a small slide, a growing line forming behind her as other children waited for their turn.

"Uh, excuse me? Can I go first?"

Suddenly, a small boy who looked to be the same age as her poked her shoulder.

"M-Mhm!" agreed Lilian, eager for the chance to delay her turn even further.

"Thanks!"

Lilian stepping aside, the boy stood in the same spot as Lilian and she noticed that his knees were shaking too. In fact, his whole body was trembling.

"Eh? Aiden? What are you doing up there!" Yelled a man from below. "You're too big of a chicken to be up on the slide! Get down!"

"I-I'm not a chicken!" replied Aiden defiantly, as he yelled back down, his shaking not lessening but in fact worsening as he shuffled forwards.

"Oh, really? Then do it!" challenged the man with a big smile.

"I will!!"

Glaring at his father, Aiden gripped the tiny bar and without thinking, threw himself onto the slide, generating more momentum than he had intended.

But despite the boy going down, screaming, Lilian couldn't help but be impressed by his bravery to do what she couldn't.

"Can I go next?" asked another boy, who seemed a bit older and more confident with going on the slide.

"I-I'll go down." Replied Lilian as she gripped the pole, the other child taking a step back, frustrated but polite enough not to argue.

Looking down at her mom, Lilian sat on the slide and closed her eyes as she went down and before she knew it, she was at the bottom.

That was when she heard sniffling, and as she opened her eyes, she saw the boy from earlier, with blood on his knee as his father quickly attended to him.

"You're a real mess, you know that Aiden?" he laughed as he wiped off the blood.

"I'll do it again! And not hurt myself next time!"

"I don't know, you might run out of knee first!"

"I'll do it! I'll show you!"

Lilian stood up and checked her own knees and dress to see if she had hurt herself, but when she realized that she was fine, she jumped up from the slide with a smile and waved at her mom, who waved back.

"Hey! You!"

Suddenly, Aiden called over to Lilian with tears still in his eyes, but before she could respond, Aiden's father smacked him atop the head.

"That's not how you greet someone. It's 'Excuse me', Aiden."

"Ow... excuse me... "

"Y-yes?"

"How did you get down the slide without getting hurt?"

"I-I don't know... I just closed my eyes... and went down."

Putting his small hand on his chin, Aiden's brow furrowed as he thought for a moment and, after a few seconds, he jetted back up the slide, and when his turn came again, he went down with his eyes closed.

Unfortunately for him, not having vision made his descent worse as his feet were snagged by the plastic floor, and he was flung face first into the ground at the bottom.

"Ow!!"

Rubbing his face, Aiden stood up and looked at the slide with challenging eyes before trying again, and again.

Eventually, he managed to complete the simple task of going down a slide unscathed, but the whole time he continued tried, Lilian couldn't help but stare in awe.

"Yes! Finally!!" cried out Aiden, as he threw his hands into the air, getting a laugh from his dad as he patted his back and brought out a box of bandages.

Seeing him cheer made Lilian feel like clapping and so she did, her tiny hands making a small "pattering" sound with Aiden, who took notice, giving her a victorious smile with a thumbs up.

"Thanks for the advice!" he yelled over. Surprising Lilian, who felt that her "advice" had only gotten him hurt worse. "Without you, I wouldn't have conquered this foul beast!!"

Waving his arms widely over the slide, Lilian couldn't help but laugh as she watched the boy continue to celebrate his achievement. She had never seen someone look so happy over something so simple.

"So, hey! My name is Aiden!" said that boy as he jogged toward Lilian. "… I think I could learn a lot from you, want to be friends?"

Reaching his hand out, Lilian looked at him with a confused look, but found it hard to resist the bandage and dirt covered boy, so with a small nod she took his hand.

"Woo! So, what's yer name?"

"L-Lilian… "

"Can I call you Lily?"

"I-if you want… "

After that day, Lilian and Aiden would begin to spend a lot of time together at the playground and eventually, places like the pool or each other's homes as their parents began talking to each other.

Their bond continuing to grow as time flew by.

His audacity inspired her, his optimism moved her. His smile seemed to be permanent and his heart of gold was why she continued to follow him after that one day. So, she could one day be like him.

And this admiration for the boy who was Aiden continued as the years passed, the boy who always kept trying no matter what. Who pushed forward in life in an endless pursuit of excellence.

But one day. That state of being, that mantle, was dropped. Never to be picked back up again by the man who once brandished it so proudly.

Leaving Lilian no choice but to pick it up herself. In hopes that Aiden would take it again one day.

This was what marked the beginning for the Lilian everyone now knew.

The Lilian whose beauty was unmatched.

The Lilian who lost to no one and the Lilian who worked hard every day without rest.

19

CLASH OF WILL

"So, this is what it took." Whispered Lilian as she slammed her axe into the ground. A feeling of jubilance rushing through her body.

The man standing in front of her had a determined face and eyes full of blazing, ferocious passion. A smile on his lips that made her feel like she was back on that playground, watching him take on the slide so many years ago.

"Is that all you have Lilian! Is that the extent of what you have to show me?!"

Throwing her axe around, Lilian lunged toward Aiden with a cocky grin on her lips and with his own arrogance filled face, he met her half way, their weapons clashing with each other. Creating an explosion of fire and wind that whipped around them.

"*Reforge yourself. With the flames of the Lord of Fire!!*" roared Ignatious triumphantly within Aiden's mind. The fire around the young man flaring up even higher.

Aiden let his spirit burn for the first time in years. Not for someone else, not for Lilian, but for himself and, as he did, he remembered his favorite childhood catchphrase.

"Lilian, I don't think you are going to beat me."

"Why is that?"

"You can't beat someone who doesn't give up."

Aiden's smile widened as he pushed Lilian back with his swords and unleashed a rapid series of slashes toward her, which she was starting to have trouble dodging as her blood-line ability began wearing her out too much.

"I don't give up either!" replied Lilian, as she jabbed at Aiden with her axe, forcing him to back away.

Taking advantage of his pause, Lilian swung her axe in a full circle before bringing the head down onto Aiden, who caught it between his blades. The swords this time not breaking as his flames enhanced their strength.

"Then let's see who gives out first!!"

What had begun as a one-sided fight was now turning into a heated duel, which all the students present couldn't help but watch in amazement as the two friends traded blows back and forth.

Even the instructor couldn't bring himself to halt the fight despite seeing both sides getting battered, because he understood what they were feeling. The howl of his two student's warrior spirits resonated deeply with him and he watched proudly while remembering his own time fighting alongside friends.

It wasn't until much later that the two came to a standstill. Neither Aiden or Lilian giving the other a chance to breathe the whole time.

The two stared at each other while breathing heavily.

Lilian's hair was a mess by now and her outfit was barely holding itself together, but that didn't mean that Aiden made it out unscathed. In fact, his outfit was in an equally if not worst state and barely any part of his body was left ignited.

But that didn't stop either of them as they both forced their arms to lift their weapons to begin exchanging a fresh volley of blows.

"Yield!" roared Aiden as he relentlessly continued his assault.

"Never!"

The two seemed like they would continue for an eternity, their weapons breaking and reforming countless times as they attacked, blocked and missed. but suddenly, the sparring horn went off and Lilian paused mid-swing only to see Aiden falling forward, his sword hitting the ground with a clank after slipping out of his grip.

His power suddenly giving out, Aiden was surprised at the sudden fatigue that washed over him and he watched the floor get closer with his body refusing to or rather, being incapable of acting.

That was when Lilian dropped her own weapon and despite her own injuries and exhaustion, used what little strength she had left to try and catch her friend.

But the attempted motion proved to be *her* breaking point as she suddenly became lightheaded and as she dropped to her knees, a small laugh escaped her lips before she fell over right on top of Aiden, who was already unconscious.

* * *

News of their sparring match spread quickly throughout the academy, rumors quickly taking root about their "epic battle" and becoming more exaggerated with each subsequent telling.

Needless to say, they became the talk of the whole academy with both students and teachers alike showing a great deal of admiration and respect towards them.

Although a lot of it fell flat to the both of them as they ended up in the infirmary together due to the damage they'd sustained.

The level of injury they had inflicted on one another was so substantial that they couldn't immediately be healed and instead needed to spend about two days in bed recovering.

But they both took it in stride with Lilian laughing about the match, rubbing it in Aiden's face that she'd won by default, and with Aiden promising to win the next one.

This sudden fame also came with the garnering of haters in Aiden's case, while like usual, Lilian only gathered admirers.

Although neither Aiden nor Lilian seemed to care as they enjoyed each other's company in the infirmary. Be it through occasionally talking or simply sitting in silence.

A deep understanding somehow now connected the two that wasn't there before, as if by crossing blades, they now knew more about each other than ever before, despite years and years of friendship growing up together.

"Despite the level of recklessness you two displayed in the training arena, the council has decided not to punish you but instead commend your spirits which they feel exemplify what it means to be a Hunter."

On the second day, right before they were discharged, a Hunter with a "back up" body, approached them with a clipboard.

Unlike most of the Hunters who wore masks to mimic their real faces, this Hunter in particular simply kept the robotic visage, not seeing the point in lamenting a form now forever lost.

"As such, the council has decided to promote Hunter Aiden to a silver border." Continued the Hunter. "And Hunter Lilian is being promoted to a platinum border. A rare honor, but one the council has decided you are worthy to receive due to the potential you have displayed in such a short time."

"Why just me? Aiden almost beat me, he should be a platinum border just like me!" complained Lilian.

"Hunter Lilian, you have taken very well to everything we teach here. Techniques, combat, theory and while Hunter Aiden is your equal in all intellect based subjects, in combat, after careful review of the match by the council, it was decided he only held his ground because you allowed yourself to be worn out too much. At your full power, Hunter Aiden would have lost indefinitely."

"That's not true... " replied Lilian as she tried to get up.

Aiden put his arm up to stop Lilian from standing and he shook his head as Lilian looked at him with a small frown.

"He's right. Even I could tell you were going easy on me at first." Smiled Aiden. "But at the end, you were giving it your all and that makes me happy to know. Next time, go all out from the start and I'll prove to them I can keep up."

"As inspiring as that is, Hunter Aiden. Unfortunately, sparring is not the place to be going 'all out'. It is training. If you wish to go 'all out' against fellow Hunters, you will need to enter the tournament we are hosting in a few months."

The Hunter took out two pieces of paper and handed one to each of them.

"The Council would like you both to participate, to show old Hunters that our organization has a bright future. There has been talk and considerable concern lately surrounding the

220

new Hunters. The Council wishes to silence this descent in the 'Grand Hunt'."

"So… will we be fighting other students and trainees?" Asked Aiden, as he read through the rules and prizes.

"No, all Hunters, regardless of age or status will be allowed to participate. Which is why it is a perfect opportunity to prove yourself. But, don't worry. If you can make it to at least the top 50%, the council will be satisfied. No one expects rookies to make it far after all. We just want to show that there are quality Hunters amongst this new group."

"I'm not particularly interested, but if Aiden participates, I will too." Declared Lilian as she put the flyer on a nearby desk.

"Is it life-threatening?"

"No, but there have been instances of Hunters pushing themselves too hard and ending up hurt. So I can't say it's a completely risk free event. Like all combat related things, there is a certain level of danger involved."

"…I'd like to participate."

"Very well, we will submit your forms. I wish you the best of luck, just try not overexert yourself. Tournaments give you a chance to show off your strength against other Hunters, but you should always remember our primary duty is to defend this humanity."

Nodding once, the Hunter left the room, and Aiden looked at the paper again, interested in the prize.

"Lone wolf status... diamond border... and a 'mystery cash prize'."

"Sounds nice, doesn't it?" smiled Lilian, as she hopped over to Aiden's bed, looking over his shoulder at his paper.

"Mhm. But I doubt we will win. We are facing off against Hunters that have years of experience."

"True, if the books are right. We are no match for these guys. Like, at all."

"Well, we did just start learning a few weeks ago." Laughed Aiden.

"But we've made a lot of progress."

"Yeah, but I know I'm still a beginner when it comes to swordsmanship. Personally, I think it would have been best to learn how to use one sword before two, but... what do I know?"

"Well, I'm a beginner too!" smiled Lilian as she bounced off the bed and grabbed her paper. "If you are serious about being a Hunter and fighting the 'paranormal', then lets both do our best to train for this tournament!"

Sticking her hand out to help Aiden up, Lilian suddenly flicked her head to the side as she felt a strange, almost malicious pair of eyes on her that reminded her of those of a predator.

Lilian searched the room while bringing Aiden to his feet, scanning all the nooks and crannies, but she couldn't find the source of that strange sensation, nor any trace of another individual being in the room with them.

It was a fairly empty room after all which had too much open space for someone to hide in. Which eventually led her to believe that she had imagined the phenomenon.

"Everything alright, Lilian?"

"Yeah."

Sparing one last look before leaving the room, Lilian closed the door behind her, having missed the subtle glint of yellow hanging around in the darker corner of the room.

20

NEW PACK

The day their time at the academy ended, Lilian and Aiden walked out wearing new Hunter outfits.

Now considered official Hunters and not "trainees" any longer, their outfits all matched and their individual ranks were only shown through a badge that could be deployed as a projection from their palms.

In the end, Aiden was given the rank of "Silver Gamma", while Lilian was deemed to be a "Platinum Gamma" although the instructor had told her that if she did well on her first few assignments, she might get promoted to Bronze or even Silver Delta.

Which was a huge honor in a system which consisting of four distinct ranks.

Those ranks being Gamma, Delta, Beta, and Alpha. With Bronze, Silver, Gold, and Platinum designating authority within said ranks.

While there were also rankings such as Lone wolf or Omega, those were very special designations that very few ever got or were even considered for. Similarly, being given Diamond status automatically granted someone the highest battlefield authority, but was unheard of for anyone outside of an Alpha to get.

"So, you survived the Academy. Well done."

At the front gate of the academy, Rosalia stood, waiting with her arms crossed. Her face more or less neutral but somewhat amused as she noticed Lilian's glare.

"And what perhaps, brings you here, Ms. Rosalia?" Asked Lilian, as she stepped in front of her.

"It just so happens that you will be stationed with me."

"What?"

"It makes sense. You live in a low-impact area, it's perfect for training, except for that one incident a few weeks ago. It seems the Council has decided for us to form a team."

"What!?"

Throwing her hands up in the air, Lilian seemed outraged at the thought of working with Rosalia, but as Aiden pulled her back, she calmed down as he took the front.

"Sorry, I guess she's still sore about whatever it is you two fought about." Apologized Aiden.

"Well, it's actually qui… "

"We don't speak of it!" declared Lilian with a finger pointed at Rosalia. "Never speak of it!"

"Fine. Anyways, it seems we will be working together. Which works out well, since your paranormal research club could be a very useful 'headquarters'. "

"I guess so."

"I don't like this."

"Well, we are all members of the same 'pack' now, so eventually, we will need to let bygones be bygones." Said Rosalia, as she offered her hand to Lilian.

Lilian looked at her hand, deep in conflict about accepting it, but as she looked at Aiden who gave her a "shake her hand" look, she eventually relented and they shook hands graciously.

"I suppose since we are all on the same team now…"

"Mhm. Let's do our best to complete our duties."

"And hopefully not die." Added Aiden.

"Yes. That would be preferable." Finished Rosalia, with a small smile.

Then, from behind Rosalia another familiar face appeared, which sent a chill down Aiden's back and caused Lilian to step forward with her arm held out defensively.

Standing calmly next to the red-haired Hunter was one certain violet haired nun, with her habit and full outfit on. She presented a warm smile to the duo as if this was the first time she had met them and bowed deeply at the two, with her body pointing significantly more towards Aiden.

"This is Catarina Ekatarina. She is a member of the Ignati Church and is being moved to our town of Lubris to provide support for us."

"She… what?!" stammered Lilian, as she instinctively started wrapping her arms around Aiden.

"The church has supported the Hunters since their founding by the Elemental Lord Ignatious. Catarina will help us organize ourselves for missions and during missions. I've been told she is one of the most promising nuns here. So, she will be accompanying us for experience."

"W… why not somewhere else?"

"It was the church's decision that I be placed at Lubris, Madam Hunter." Replied Catarina, with a smile. "To get used to supporting Hunters and perhaps cement a more permanent spot among your ranks after gaining your trust."

Catarina's eyes focused on Aiden as she finished her sentence and Lilian glared at her in response, causing the nun's focus to shift back to the upset Lilian.

"It's fine." Whispered Aiden in Lilian's ear. "I'm sure everything will be fine."

Letting out a sigh, Lilian walked past the both of them and towards the transport that was supposed to take them back home.

"Let's go then."

"Let's." replied Rosalia. "Our first assignment as a 'pack' will be to take care of an 'aspect of pestilence' that has appeared in the city."

"Oh, nice! Our first assignment! How are we going to battle it? Night? Do I need silver, gold? Or holy water?" asked Aiden eagerly, as he made his way over to the car with the rest of the group.

"We will battle it with cleaning."

"Oh! I see Clea... wait, what?!"

"Yup. Not all paranormal entities can be 'killed'. Some of them need to be quite literally cleaned. We can kill the form it takes as many times as we want, but as long as the 'dirty spot' remains, it'll simply return as soon as we 'kill' it."

"Eehhh? I spent this much time training only to become a maid?" complained Aiden bitterly as Lilian pulled him into the car.

"It wasn't that long. The Academy showed you the basics, it's up to you to survive and expand on those basics. Unfortunately, one can only learn to be a Hunter through hands-on experience."

Sitting in the passenger seat, with Aiden in the back between Lilian and Catarina, Rosalia took out a pair of sunglasses and put them on her face before looking back.

"So, be sure to get some cleaning equipment and we will begin. Some citizens have gotten sick and while they haven't reached a state of it being fatal, the cities starting to slow down out of fear of a pandemic starting to spread. "

"Alright."

The engine of the car roaring to life, Aiden gripped his cloak with a repressed smile as he looked out the window.

The bright horizon shone more brilliantly than he could remember and as he watched the sun rise high into the sky, he couldn't help but appreciate the beauty of it more then he did in the past.

The Hunters were real. All his time reading wasn't for naught. All his studying and hours had finally bore fruit which was evidenced by the golden crest now sitting on his chest.

And as the next chapter of the organization's history began, Aiden was excited to know that he was going to be there as witness and perhaps even a writer himself.